Renata, A Child of the Holocaust

A Novel Based on the Life of Renata Haberer

Helen Stein Behr

Cover Design: M. Masters

Printed in the United States of America.

This is a work of fiction, based on the life of Renata Haberer. A portion of all proceeds will be donated to the Simon Wiesenthal Center in the memory of Renee Krauss and her family.

ISBN-10: 1512374512

ISBN-13: 978-1512374513

DEDICATION

To all the children of the Holocaust.

ACKNOWLEDGMENTS

There are many people I wish to thank, who were essential to the completion of this book.

I am grateful to my daughter Susan Stein Koehler who spent countless hours in seeing this book through to its completion.

I am also grateful to Ellen Stein for graciously proofreading this book.

I also want to thank Bob Stein, Melissa Solomon, Amelia Stein and Ted Stein for their ongoing support and assistance.

And of course, I want to thank Renee Krauss, who shared her amazing story with me.

CONTENTS

1. Renata 1944 *1*
2. Changes in the Wind *4*
3. The Nuremberg Laws *10*
4. The Night of Broken Glass *14*
5. Beyond Kristallnacht *26*
6. Deportation *33*
7. The Train Ride *40*
8. Le Camp de Gurs *45*
9. Gustel Haberer *52*
10. A Sad Farewell *56*
11. Aspet *60*
12. On To Limoges *63*
13. Another Farewell *72*
14. Crossing to Safety *78*
15. Switzerland *84*
16. 1945 *93*

Postscript *98*

About the Book *109*

CHAPTER 1

RENATA 1944

Huddled in her bed, with tears running down her cheeks, 10-year-old Renata Haberer tried to bury her face in the pillow so no one could hear her sobs. She didn't want anyone to know how she was feeling—except for her mama and papa.

All she wanted was her mama and papa. She wanted them to hold her tight, to love her and tell her that everything would be all right. Is that too much for her to wish for? Why was she growing up without her family?

How she hated the boarding school in which her relatives had placed her. She especially hated Fraulein Eichorn. She hated Switzerland, even though it was so beautiful.

Fraulein Eichorn should never have been put in charge of children. Renata felt that the Fraulein hated them all, but she particularly hated the children who could not speak proper German.

All day the Fraulein had been screaming at everyone.

But tonight, she really had taken it out on Renata's best friend, Hannah.

Hannah had come from Poland. One day, she'd come home from school and her family was just gone. That same day, some kind neighbors quickly packed a small suitcase of clothes for her and brought her to a safe house for Jews. She was then taken to Switzerland. The neighbors had explained that this was the only way to keep a Polish Jewish girl safe. Hannah never heard from her family or neighbors again.

Tonight was Hannah's turn to wash the dishes. She had left a spot on one of the plates. Fraulein Eichorn was so furious; she slapped Hannah hard across the face leaving red finger marks on her cheek. The blow had made the frightened girl drop the plate and it had smashed into smithereens. The broken plate enraged the woman so much, she screamed even more. The Fraulein yelled at Hannah, telling her she was a worthless child. She yelled that Hannah couldn't even speak German properly. Of course she couldn't! Hannah came from Poland. Could the Fraulein speak Polish? Life is so unfair, Renata thought. "Mama," she cried to herself. "I need you to help me understand why I am here, in a strange country, far from the people that I love. Oh mama, oh papa—I need you both so much!"

The sobs finally subsided, as her eyes grew heavy. She recalled what mama had told her to do when she was feeling lonesome: I'll close my eyes, she told herself, and then I can see papa and mama and Opa and Oma and my little sister Ellen. Renata pictured them sitting around the table. There was hot chocolate topped with whipped cream in white china cups. There were crusty rolls spread with sweet cherry preserves. She could almost feel the thick rich chocolate sliding down her throat. She could hear her papa's deep voice, see his twinkling blue eyes and her mama's sweet smile. And with that, Renata finally drifted off to sleep.

CHAPTER 2

CHANGES IN THE WIND

When she woke the next morning, her thoughts went back to her past. How her life had changed! It had happened so gradually that she had not even noticed. She realized that her parents had tried to keep her childhood as normal as possible.

Now she wanted to know how Germany had changed so radically under the Nazi government. When had the German Jews stopped being German citizens and become only "subjects" in Hitler's Reich? When did "Jew" become a horrible word? Her parents' had always thought of themselves, first as Germans, and being Jewish was simply observing their faith in their God.

Renata knew that both her parents had been born in Germany and her mother's family had lived in Germany for more than four hundred years. Their family was forced to leave Spain for Germany in 1492, because they were Jewish. Renata's family had lived in Germany, established a thriving manufacturing business, even fought and given their lives for Germany.

Renata recalled the story her papa, Gustel Haberer, had told her about World War I. Her papa had been only sixteen when his older brother was killed in the Great War. When papa heard the tragic news, he felt there had to be a Haberer fighting for his country. Taking his brother's birth certificate, Gustel rushed out of the house to enlist. Renata wondered, didn't that prove that he was a loyal German?

Her own dear Opa, mama's papa, had fought in World War I. Opa had saved all his comrades during a siege. While rescuing them, he had been hit by a shell and lost his eye. As soon as he was discharged from the hospital, he insisted on returning to the front lines. For his bravery, he had been awarded The Iron Cross (Germany's highest field honor).

When Hitler came to power, none of this seemed to matter. Renata trembled when she thought of Hitler, the Gestapo, the Brown Shirts, and the dreadful cruelty happening in Germany.

Looking back on her childhood, Renata recalled her happy, carefree life as a little girl. She remembered her beautiful town of Offenburg, the red roofs, the towering church steeple, and best of all, the train station. In the past, trains had fascinated her.

Renata had thought about the first house she had lived in until she was four, in Offenburg, Germany. It was a large, lovely villa in a beautiful garden setting. Her mama loved flowers and had planted one of the loveliest gardens in town. While she had been too young to know the names of the flowers, she could never forget the profusion of bright reds, sweet pinks, the cheerful yellows and dazzling whites. She could almost breathe in the delicious fragrances that enveloped her as she sat under her special tree-shaded place. It was under the shadow of this tree that she would sit with Albert, her most beloved teddy bear, and sing and tell him stories.

Then, in her memory, she entered the house. To the right, there was a large salon (living room); to the left was the dining room, a room where large family dinners took place. On Rosh Hashanah, the Jewish New Year, there would be sweet and sour fish, sauerbraten and, best of all, her favorite dessert, *mohrenkopf*. (*Mohrenkopf* is a gooey cream covered with chocolate.) Her mouth watered as she thought of it. It had been way too long since she had tasted one. There were other delicious cakes and candy to welcome the New Year. Sounds of happy voices and peals of laughter filled the room. "A Good *Yontif* (A Happy Holiday) to you all," was said and repeated over and over again.

Renata then thought of the springtime holiday of Passover. At this time the family gathered around the table for the Seder. The Seder is the Passover service accompanied by a feast that commemorates the exodus of the Jewish slaves from Egypt. A snow-white tablecloth covered the table, and sparkling crystal goblets were filled with dark red wine. The candles glowed as her family and close friends retold the miraculous story of the holiday. But mostly, Renata remembered the laughter and singing after the tale was told. Now she realized the importance of that story, and wished that she had listened more closely. Back then, it was a warm, wonderful feeling being a Jewish girl!

Renata sighed deeply, and in her mind, continued walking through her house. Past the dining room, and past her papa's office, she came to the sewing room. Her face lit up at the thought of that cozy, cheerful room. This was where she and her mama spent so many happy hours. Her mama loved to sew, and while she was sewing, Renata would sit on a small stool close by. As the machine sang its monotonous song, her mama would tell her stories. The stories Renata loved best were the ones of her mama's childhood. Mama told her of her house in Bergen. She talked about her toys, friends, and special times.

Renata loved hearing about the *Wandergruppen*, or excursion group, to which her mama, like most young Germans, belonged. The group went on long hikes in the mountains and forests. Mama described the beauty of the German countryside. She sang the songs they had sung as they hiked, and Renata, or Rena, as she was often called, could hardly wait until she would be old enough to join. She now knew that this would never happen.

Best of all, Renata loved hearing about the *Schultüte*, a huge cone filled with candy. All children received one when they entered kindergarten. Renata was filled with delight at the thought of so much candy! While she was a terrible eater, her appetite was insatiable for candy and other sweets. Renata's first day of school was terribly disappointing, as she had never received a *Schultüte*.

She thought of the rest of the house - the kitchen, the bedrooms where the cook and the maid slept. She then climbed the stairs to her bedroom with her four-poster princess bed. It was so high; she had to step on a stool to reach it. It was given to her as a surprise when her little sister, Ellen, was born. Her papa had told her that she could keep it forever. She wondered ruefully what little girl was sleeping in it now!

In her mind's eye, she peeked into her nanny's room, her parent's bedroom and the nursery. She went up another flight of stairs to the attic, which contained her mother's old clothes, toys, and other mementos of her mother's childhood. Renata enjoyed dressing up in those clothes and playing house with her friends and cousins.

She missed her house, but most of all she missed her family. Her father was tall, handsome and strong. He had black hair, a big bushy mustache and his blue eyes would often crinkle in laughter. He loved to pick up Renata and dance around the room with her. When the family went to the Synagogue, Renata would sit upstairs with the women and other girls. She would gaze down at the men praying. Her eyes quickly found her tall papa. She knew that he was the most handsome man in the temple – especially in his tallis, the prayer shawl that the Jewish men wore at services. His tallis had a wide blue stripe embroidered in silver thread. She had been so proud of him.

How beautiful her sweet mama was with her soft dark eyes and her wavy black hair. Her mama's eyes were filled with understanding, and her arms were forever beckoning Renata with love and comfort.

There was her loving Oma and Opa, her aunts and uncles, cousins and friends. There were so many people for her to love.

Now, there was her baby sister, Ellen. Renata had not wanted her parents to have a baby. Her parents tried to convince her how wonderful it would be to have a brother or sister, but she was not thrilled about having to share her mama and papa. But wanting to please her parents, she told them that she would be happy to be a big sister.

Her father told her that if she really wanted a baby, she would have to help the stork. She was to set out a sugar cube on the windowsill for the stork every night. And when the stork had enough sugar, he would bring the Haberer's a new baby.

Renata dutifully set out a sugar cube every night, and one November morning, her papa came to her room, sat on the edge of the bed and took Rena on his lap. "Because you were such a good girl, and remembered to put out a sugar cube each night, the stork has brought you a sister."

"Oh no, Papa," Renata confessed, "I put out a sugar

cube every night, but then, I ate it."

"Well Rena," grinned her father, "I guess he brought you one anyway."

How lucky I am to have Ellen now, thought Renata. She is the only one of my family in Switzerland with me. Not that she is physically with me, but at least I know that she is not far away.

Nevertheless, in those early days, having a baby around simply was not great. Ellen was an exceptionally beautiful baby with dark curls, and Renata did not relish all of the attention that the baby received.

With dark straight hair and lively brown eyes, Renata *was* an adorable and charming little girl. Her winning smile and interest in people made her easily loved, even by Ellen. Finally, Renata found a reason to love Ellen. She discovered that Ellen could be used as her human garbage pail. Renata was a terrible eater. She hated cereal, vegetables, meat and even fruit. Her mama tried to impress upon her that she should eat so that she could become big and strong. She told her how lucky she was to have food. There were so many children who were starving, but Renata didn't see how her eating would help them. She wished that she could give them her food. Needless to say, mealtimes were not a pleasant experience.

One day, she made a startling discovery. She found that if she secretly gave Ellen her food, she would happily eat it. Unlike Renata, Ellen loved to eat. Her mother had always strained Ellen's food, so the baby did not have to chew her food. But Ellen didn't care, and simply ate all the food that Renata gave her.

Renata always asked to sit near Ellen. The baby adored her big sister and mama was glad that Renata wanted to sit near her. She was also happy that Renata was eating more wholesome foods. Now everyone was happy!

CHAPTER 3

THE NUREMBERG LAWS

In January, 1933, after Hitler was appointed Chancellor, Jews became known as *Untermenschen* or inferior people. Jews were no longer allowed to go to restaurants, theaters, concerts, movies or swimming pools. Jews were only allowed to sit on designated yellow park benches. Also, in 1933, there was a boycott of Jewish stores. German people were not allowed to buy from Jewish-owned stores. The Nuremberg Laws, which were passed in 1935, stated that the Jewish People were no longer citizens of Germany. Jews were forbidden to employ German women under the age of 45. But Renata was too young to realize how this would affect her life. She reminisced that one day her father's car was just gone. She hadn't known that Hitler had issued an order that Jews could no longer own cars. When she found her family no longer had a car, she had happily exclaimed, "Now we can always ride the trains!" And, yes, she had liked that idea.

She hadn't understood her father's sad smile as he said, "It's good to have you around, my little Renamaus. Nothing ever seems as bad when you are here."

It certainly wasn't a happy event when they had to move from their big house. Nevertheless, she felt much better when she heard that her Oma and Opa were going to live with them. Of course, now Renata knew they had to give up their house because a Nazi in town wanted to live in their villa. Her grandparents had moved in with them because Jews could no longer have an apartment for just one family. A Jewish family was only permitted to have two rooms. Renata brooded, "All I could think of then was that my Oma, with her wonderful stories, and my Opa, who played such fun games, would be living with me. I was so dumb."

Renata had actually enjoyed living in the apartment house. She liked visiting people and made friends with the neighbors in the building. She really liked the Kramers, who lived on the top floor. They had a candy dish that was always full of raspberry candies filled with soft centers. She was extremely fond of those candies. Herr and Frau Kramer often filled her hands with them.

The Buhlers, a mother and grown daughter whose name was also Renata, lived downstairs. Although the young woman was a Nazi, and even worked for the Gestapo in Stuttgart, she liked little Renata very much. She would often take her for walks and buy her little presents. Once she took Renata to have her picture taken by a German photographer. At that time, Renata did not understand her mother's alarm when she had noticed her daughter's picture in the window of the photography store. Jews were not allowed to have their pictures taken by German photographers. If it had been discovered, who knew what might have happened. Years later, Renata understood her mother's concern.

Renata now realized that although she visited her neighbors, her parents and grandparents did not. Nor did the other non-Jewish tenants come to the Haberers.

The Haberers' family and friends started leaving Germany. Fearful of the future, they left for safe havens. Her favorite Aunt Martha and her fiancé Ludwig got visas for South Africa, permitting them to emigrate. Renata remembered that very clearly. She had been so unhappy that she tried to prevent it from happening. Her family had gone to see her aunt in Frankfurt, to say their farewells. When Renata saw her aunt's clothes set out for the following day's departure, she asked, "Is that what you are wearing tomorrow?" "Yes." answered her aunt. "Is everything else packed?" questioned Renata. "Yes," her aunt replied. Renata took her aunt's stockings and plunged them under the running water in the sink.

"Now," she told her aunt, "you won't be able to go, because you have no stockings to wear."

Her aunt held her close and said, "I will miss you too Rena, I love you so much and some day, we will be together again."

The stockings eventually dried and Martha left as planned. Renata did not know if she would ever see her beloved aunt again.

Many others left Germany as well, but Renata's father felt that Hitler would not remain in power, and until that time, he thought that he could keep his family safe.

"Oh, if we had only gone to America, when our cousins in New York asked us, we would have been spared all this."

However, the Haberers had chosen to remain in Germany. In 1938, she was only five years old and her parents protected her, and kept her from realizing the whole truth. Like all five year olds, she played and sang, and if her world was shrinking, she never knew it. As long as she was with her family, life was good.

CHAPTER 4

THE NIGHT OF BROKEN GLASS

On November 9, 1938, came *Kristallnacht* (the night of broken glass). This was the day the Nazis ran through the town breaking windows of Jewish owned establishments so that broken glass littered the streets. In addition they looted and destroyed as many Jewish businesses and synagogues as they could. This infamous night was the night that changed everything for the Jews. This night was a turning point: their hope that things would improve ceased to exist.

Loud banging and angry shouts awakened Renata. She ran from her bedroom to the front hall. Two soldiers with pointed guns stood there.

"Gustel Haberer and Julius Strauss (her Opa), you are to come. Get dressed—*schnell schnell!* (fast fast) Who else is in the house with you?" one soldier shouted.

"My wife and two children and our maid Anna," Renata's father replied.

"Does anyone else live here?"

"My mother-in-law, but she is visiting relatives right now."

"Is the maid Jewish?"

"No," Gustel said in a low voice.

Anna, dressed only in her robe, had come into the hall and had taken Renata's hand. The soldier looked at her contemptuously. "And you work for Jews?" he sneered. "It is no longer permitted for Aryans to work for Jews! You are to leave immediately."

Gustel pleaded, "My wife is ill. She has a high fever. She can't be alone with two small children. Please, can't the maid remain at least until my mother-in–law returns?"

The soldiers continued to point their guns. Anna had no choice but to leave. She squeezed Renata's hand and went to get her things.

Renata stood trembling, looking from her papa to the soldiers. How could anyone order her papa around? He was always in charge!

Seeing her frightened face, papa said, "Renamaus, it will be alright."

Somewhat reassured, always believing that her papa knew everything, she felt a little better.

Just then Opa Julius came into the room, holding his Iron Cross, the medal he had won for bravery in the First World War.

"You can't take that!" the first soldier yelled.

The other soldier, who seemed kinder and even a little embarrassed said, "Let him take it. It's his. Now, *schnell*, get dressed!"

Opa left the room.

When he returned, he was dressed in his full First World War uniform. He stood straight and tall, in knee-high boots. He wore a big belt around his hip-length, brass-buttoned jacket. His Iron Cross and other medals were pinned to his jacket.

"You can't come in a uniform," shouted the first soldier.

"It's his. Let him alone. Come on, we've spent too much time here already."

Renata ran to her father. "It's only for a little while, Renamaus. Be a good girl and help your mama." He bent and kissed her goodbye.

She then ran into her mama's room, where her mother was lying in bed, too weak from the high fever to even sit up. With great effort, Ruth propped herself up on her pillow, and put her arms around her small daughter.

"Rena honey, don't be frightened. Papa and Opa will be back soon."

"Rena," she continued, "listen carefully, because what I am about to tell you is very important. Bad things are happening to the Jewish people now. I want you to know that it is not because God is punishing us. The Jews are doing nothing wrong. But there are some bad people in our country who are doing it, and someday they will be punished. Renata, the Jews are doing nothing wrong!"

Ruth was acutely aware that Renata had been sheltered from their radically changing world. She needed Renata to completely understand.

"But right now, we have to work things out. As you know, Anna had to leave, so you and I have to figure out how Ellen, you and I will eat. I can't get out of bed, so what do you think you can do? You can't light the stove."

"Yes I can," Renata replied very sure of herself. "No you can't," her mother stated firmly. "Well," Renata said thoughtfully, giving up the exciting idea of using matches to light the stove, "I can get food from the ice box. I can climb up and reach the bread. I can do that."

"Good, do you know the hot plate that I use to heat Ellen's milk?"

"Yes, mama, it's in the kitchen cupboard. I can climb up and reach that too."

Renata went downstairs to the kitchen and she pulled a chair over to the cupboard and carefully climbed on the chair so that she could reach the bread and hot plate. She then took milk, cheese and butter from the icebox. After all this was done, she brought them all to her mama's bed. This took several trips for the young child because she was not able to carry more than a few things at one time.

"Now, Renata, we need a knife. Do you know where Papa keeps his pocket knife?"

"Mama, I know how to carry a regular knife. Anna taught me when I would help her cook. You hold it by the handle with the sharp edge down."

"Good, little one, be very, very careful. Bring a knife to me, and be sure to walk slowly."

Renata did as she was told.

"We only have one other problem; I don't know what to do about Ellen," her mama Ruth said softly to herself.

"Ellen is so young and really can't eat bread and cheese. I am too weak to get out of bed and strain her baby food. I don't know what to do."

"But mama, she can eat regular food. She can eat bread and cheese."

"You know that she can't. I have to strain everything she eats."

"Mama, she can!"

"How can she? What are you saying?"

Renata hung her head sheepishly. "You know how you told me that I was such a good big sister, because I always wanted Ellen to sit near me while I ate. You also said that I was getting to be a much better eater too."

"What?" mama demanded, nervous as to where all this was leading.

"Well, she sat next to me and I gave her all the food that I didn't want to eat when you weren't looking. And

Mama, she ate it. She can. Are you very mad at me?"

Renata's mama smiled and looked toward heaven. "*Lieber* God," (Dear God) she whispered, "you know more than we do."

"Well Renata, I will forgive you this time, but no more lies. Now eat your bread and cheese, and drink your milk. All of it, while I am watching! Then I want you to try to get Ellen out of her crib."

Renata ate everything without complaint. When she had finished, her mother said, "Now go to Ellen's crib. Look at the bottom of the crib. There is a little bar that you have to push so that the side of the crib will go down. Try it, Rena."

Renata went over to the crib and found the bar. Try as she might, her fingers were too small and weak to release the catch. She went to her mother for further instructions. But, her mama's eyes were closed. Renata knew how sick she was, so she decided to let her sleep, while she cared for her baby sister. She took the baby's bottle, which her mama had already prepared, and some bread and cheese. Handing Ellen the bottle, she sat quietly by the side of the crib, while Ellen finished her milk. Then Ellen stood up, threw the bottle on the floor, looked at Renata and said, "Down."

Renata couldn't lift her. She thought for a minute and then decided to climb into the crib so that she could feed Ellen, and play with her.

Ellen gladly ate the bread and cheese. She was delighted to see Renata in her crib. They played for a while and Renata got another idea. She would teach Ellen how to climb out. Very patiently, she showed the one and a half year old Ellen, how to put her legs over the top railing of the crib and then slowly slide down the crib bars. When the girls' mother opened her eyes, both children were sitting beside her on her bed.

"How did Ellen get out? Did you lower the side?"

"No, but I did teach her how to climb out by herself."

"How will she get back in?"

"I will teach her that too."

Now, her mother thought, my peace is gone. I will never know where Ellen is.

Again, Renata worked at teaching her little sister to climb, this time into her crib.

That afternoon, Frau Buhler, the neighbor who lived on the floor below them, rang their bell. Although, it was dangerous to help her Jewish neighbors, Frau Buhler felt there were things she, as a good person, had to do. Renata answered the door, and brought the woman to her mother's room. "Frau Haberer," she asked, "is there anything that I can do for you?"

Renata's mother answered, "No thank you very much; we can manage. Rena is a big help to me. I do appreciate your offering, but I don't want you to get into any trouble because of me."

Relieved, Frau Buhler left.

Luckily, that afternoon, many of the Jewish women of the town walked to the Haberers' home. Aware of Frau Haberer's illness, they brought food. Dr. Weigand, a Jewish woman doctor, also brought what little medication she still had, to help bring the fever down. The women changed and bathed Ellen and then did whatever was necessary around the apartment. After the women left, the three Haberers were able to manage until Oma returned.

A few days after Oma returned, Anna came back to work for the Haberers. Anna had found out that since she was older than 45, she could work for a Jewish family.

The household started to function normally. The men were gone, but Renata's mama was better, Oma and Anna were there and five-year-old Renata returned to her play and books. For long periods of time she could forget that Papa and Opa were still not home.

Ellen's birthday came and went. No Papa! No Opa!

"Mama, will Papa be back for my birthday? It's almost here."

"Let's hope so. You know Papa will be here if he possibly can."

The men of Offenburg started returning. On November 30, three weeks after *Kristallnacht*, the first group of men came home. Her Papa's cousin Robert was among them. "How's my Papa?" Renata asked.

"Oh, he is fine," cousin Robert replied, a little uncomfortably. No one even told Frau Haberer the truth until Opa returned.

It was a happy day when Julius Strauss, Renata's Opa, returned. He kissed his wife, daughter and his two grandchildren. Then he murmured to his daughter, "Ruth, I want to speak to you alone."

"What, Papa?" she cried. "Is it about Gustel?" He put his finger on his lips. Renata noticed this and became alarmed. Renata cried out, "Where is my Papa? Why isn't he home?"

Opa said, "I'll talk to you soon, Rena, but right now I have to speak to your Mama."

Oma turned to her granddaughter. "Come, Rena, I need you to help me. We're going to make a special dinner for Opa tonight to welcome him home." Distracted, Rena went with her Oma.

Opa took Ruth into the living room, "Tell me quickly, is Gustel okay?"

"Let me talk. First of all, I want you to know that your husband is a very courageous man."

Ruth, fearfully interrupted, "Papa, please tell me, where is Gustel?"

"Let me tell you in my own way. I've had so much time to think, and there are some things that I want to say to you. Ruth, remember the day when you were only 19 and came home from your cousin Robert's house? Your eyes were shining and you carried a huge bouquet of roses. I'll never forget how lovely you looked and then you told Mama and me that you were engaged. I was furious. You were so young and brilliant. I wanted you to finish school and see something of the world. But you were adamant. You cried and swore that you would become a nun if we didn't let you marry Gustel. So finally, your mother and I gave in. Very reluctantly, I might add. But Ruth, you were wise beyond your years. You could never have found a man as good and just as your Gustel. He cannot bear cruelty and injustice, and more importantly, he is not afraid to do something about it. If there were more people like him, we wouldn't have Hitler ruling our country."

"I know Papa, I know. I love him so much, but tell me, please, where is he? Why aren't you telling me? Please stop trying to protect me!" Her voice had become shrill as she needed to know, yet was afraid to learn, what had happened to Gustel.

"All the Jewish men in this area were brought to the town jail and from there, we were put on a train which took us to Dachau. It's a concentration camp near Munich. When we got there, terribly hot, blinding lights illuminated the whole camp. We were surrounded by hundreds of SS troops. They forced us to stand, without food, for eight hours, while they interviewed each man. Then they shaved our heads and beards and mustaches. We were given scalding hot showers, followed by ice-cold ones. After that, we had to put on striped prison uniforms. We were doctors, professors, men from all walks of life, honorable men being treated like the worst of criminals."

Ruth covered her eyes and gave a low sob. Her Gustel, her Papa—bald and treated so shamefully. She pulled herself together and quietly said, "Go on, Papa. Tell me the rest."

"Well, food was scarce. All we got was some watery soup, some bread, some tea. On top of that, young and old, we were made to do exercises, for hours on end. We all became very weak, but particularly, the older men. They couldn't keep up and the guards beat them when they fell from exhaustion. During one of these periods, an elderly man, whom your husband knew from childhood, stumbled and fell. A guard came to hit the old man with his rifle, and Gustel couldn't stand it. He had seen too much. He was horrified as to what was going on in this place. Though we were all helpless in this situation, Gustel couldn't control his anger any longer, and reached out and pushed the guard with all his might."

"Oh," whispered Ruth, "what did they do?"

"They made him stand outside all night in his light prison uniform. It was snowing and bitterly cold. By morning, he was frozen. One ear and an arm were frost bitten. When he was brought to the guardroom, the SS man laughed. "You're freezing, I'll help you." And he put Gustel's arm on the hot steam pipes.

Ruth gasped.

"Yes, you know what can happen. His arm became infected. They didn't give him any treatment. He was taken to the infirmary but nothing was done there. He was already weak from lack of food and he had no resources left to fight the high fever and infection."

"Is he alive?" Ruth murmured, afraid of the answer.

"Yes, but he is very, very sick. I am not at all sure he can survive. I pleaded with them, and for some inexplicable reason, they agreed to send him home. He is very ill. He is being sent home tomorrow."

When Renata heard that her father was coming home, she was very excited. She never heard her mother's warning that her Papa was terribly sick. All she heard was that he was returning in time for her sixth birthday. She couldn't wait to be picked up and thrown into the air. She couldn't wait to feel his big mustache tickle as he kissed her hello.

The next morning, she was too impatient to wait upstairs. She ran outside in that freezing winter day, and she watched each car as it came down the street. An ambulance stopped at the door of her building. Renata paid no attention to it. She was waiting for a car, but then, two men brought a man out on a stretcher.

Renata stared. It couldn't be Papa. Papa was strong. Papa had lots of thick black hair and a bushy black mustache. This man was thin and weak. He couldn't move. He had no hair and no mustache. He certainly couldn't pick up a little girl. Renata moved closer. She saw his blue eyes and heard a soft voice say, "My little Renamaus." Only her Papa called her that. He tried to raise his arm to stroke her head, but he was too weak.

Seeing this, one of the attendants lifted the little girl and placed her on the stretcher in the curve of her father's good arm. The other arm was too painful to touch. Her Mama came flying down the stairs. As she tenderly kissed him, she whispered, "We'll get you well, Gustel."

Holding his good hand and with Renata still in the crook of his arm, they slowly climbed the stairs to their apartment.

As soon as they entered their apartment, Renata ran to her room and threw herself on her bed and cried and cried. Oma came in and took her in her arms. "Rena, little one, Papa will get better. Wait, and you will see."

Rena kept as close to Oma as possible. And soon, her

terrible racking sobs stopped.

What was Frau Haberer to do? The only Jewish doctor remaining in Offenburg was Doctor Weigand, who had helped her on *Kristallnacht.* But, she had no medication to treat such a terrible infection. German doctors were forbidden to treat Jewish patients. But like her husband, Ruth Haberer was brave and determined. As soon as darkness fell, disobeying the curfew for Jews, she carefully ran through the empty streets in search of the non-Jewish doctor that the family had previously used. She hoped this doctor would have the medication that Gustel so desperately needed.

"Herr Doctor," she pleaded, "will you please come and treat my husband. I know that it is against the law. But you are a doctor and my husband will die if he isn't cared for. Please, I beg you."

The doctor looked at the weeping woman and remembered the oath that he had taken to treat the ill. "Go now, I will come to your house tonight at 11 o'clock, when it should be quiet. Leave the door open so that I will not have to ring the bell or knock."

"Thank you Herr Doctor, you really are a good man."

At precisely 11 P.M. the doctor came. He dressed the arm and gave Herr Haberer medication to fight the raging infection and fever. He continued to come in secret every night at 11 P.M., until Renata's father was out of danger.

"Your husband will be all right, Frau Haberer. Now I must ask you to never call me again, no matter what happens. I am terribly sorry, but it is putting my family in danger, and that I will not do."

"Thank you for your care this time. There is no way that I can thank you enough. I do understand and I will never bother you again."

December 23rd, Renata's sixth birthday, came and went.

There was no party, there was no celebration. It was a day spent in sadness and fear.

CHAPTER 5

BEYOND KRISTALLNACHT

Just as Oma had said, Papa did get better. He remained deaf in one ear, but his arm healed. Life took on a feeling of normalcy.

"Mama, play with me."

"I can't, Rena. I have to finish this dress that I am making for you."

"Mama, you are always busy sewing or cleaning or playing with Ellen. I need someone to play with me!"

Ruth Haberer was worried about Renata. It was true that Ellen was getting a lot of attention. She was full of happy baby gurgling and made the family forget what was happening in Hitler's Germany. Renata didn't have anything to do. In normal times, she would be attending kindergarten. But German schools were closed to Jewish children and Jewish children could only attend Jewish schools. The closest one was a train ride away in the town of Freiburg. The older children of Offenburg would travel on the train on Sunday, spend the week living in the home of a relative or friend, go to school on the weekdays, and then return home for the weekend. Renata was too young to do this, and as a result, she had nothing to do. There were no children of her age left in her town. Her days were long and empty.

"Rena," asked her Mama, "how would you like to spend some of your days with the Stein sisters?"

"Yes, Mama. I just love them and their dog Prince. Beside they always give me candy."

Her mother laughed, "You and candy! Well, I will ask them if they can do it."

The two Stein sisters were unmarried and had always loved Renata. She was the child that they never had. They had been primary school teachers in a German school and had lost their jobs. Their days, like Renata's, were empty. They were delighted to teach Renata.

"We would love to teach Renata, and it would give purpose to our days as well. Let Renata come everyday and it will be good for all of us."

So it was arranged, and Renata started to enjoy life again. Some days, the three of them would go on excursions and then Renata would write about it. Other days they would spend at home, where Rena, who had already learned to read, would read books to the sisters or dictate her own stories.

That stimulated her imagination, and when she returned home, she would proudly read her own stories to her parents. "I think I'll be a writer when I grow up," she claimed.

The days passed. War with France started and the French were bombing Germany. Offenburg was right on the border of France and Germany and the bombers came every night. Renata thought it very exciting to be awakened in the middle of the night to go down to the basement, but the parents feared for their children.

The Jewish families of Offenburg got together and

decided it would be best to move inland to Munich, until the heavy bombing ceased.

The move to Munich would solve many additional problems for the Haberers. Not only would they be away from the bombing, but also Renata would be able to attend a school with other children. Unlike the small town they lived in, Munich had enough Jews to form their own school. Best of all, Herr and Frau Haberer would be employed by the Munich Jewish Children's Home. Herr Haberer was to be in charge of purchasing and Frau Haberer would do the necessary sewing.

The extra income would help support the family. There had been no work for Herr Haberer in Offenburg. The family was living on their savings. The government only permitted a small amount of money to be withdrawn each month. In addition to supporting his family of four, Renata's father was also supporting Oma and Opa, his two sisters and their husbands, and a niece. Money was becoming a big concern.

So the four of them went to Munich. They found lodging with a Jewish man who was forced to rent out some of the rooms in his house. The villa was located in a beautiful suburb of Munich. The first thing Renata did was to go outside. She was in awe of the abundance of flower gardens.

She decided she would pick a bouquet of flowers for her Mama. It was so long since her Mama had any flowers, and flowers had always made her so happy.

"Look Mama," she said hiding the bouquet behind her. "I brought you a beautiful present."

"What is it, Rena?"

Renata brought forth the colorful flowers, but instead of the happiness that she expected, her Mama looked stunned and scared.

"Renata, where did you get those flowers?"

"I picked them for you. Don't you like them?" she whimpered.

Her Papa had entered the room and yelled, "Renata, how could you do that? You know those flowers belong to someone else! How can we trust you out of our sight?"

Her mother took her in her arms. "Listen to me, Rena, I know you meant well. I do love flowers, but Rena, we must be very careful in everything we do. If someone reported you to the police, we would be in terrible trouble. Because we are Jewish, the police will look for any excuse to arrest us. Please, *liebling*, (my love) promise us you will never ever pick flowers from anyone's garden."

Renata promised, and when she promised something, she did try to keep her word. However, one day she came home with a beautiful rose.

Her Papa got all flustered. "You promised that you would not pick anymore flowers."

"But Papa, I didn't!"

"Then where did you get that rose?"

"From our Fuhrer."

Her Papa said gravely, "I will not have you lying to me. Now tell me the truth."

Just then her mother entered the room and saw the rose.

"Where did you get this rose? We told you we could get in trouble if you pick flowers from people's gardens."

"But Mama, I didn't. I kept my promise. Our Fuhrer gave it to me."

Her mother eyed her sternly.

"Is that the truth?"

"Yes it is Mama. Ask Greta."

Greta was the maid who still worked for their Jewish landlord. She had taken a liking to Renata and had volunteered to watch her while the Haberers were working.

Frau Haberer called Greta, and asked her where the rose had come from. Greta hung her head nervously. "Frau Haberer, I am so ashamed. You know that I don't like Hitler. If I did, I wouldn't be working for a Jewish person. But today, Hitler was coming and there was going to be a big parade. I love parades and I wanted to see all the flowers and the bright colors, so I took Renata. We were standing well in the back, but before I knew it, Renata had wiggled her way to the front. It would have been more dangerous for me to get her then, so I had to leave her there until after the parade. And there she stood, waving a flag someone had given her and she caught one of the roses that were being thrown."

"Rena, Renamaus, what are we going to do with you?" her Papa wanted to know.

"Are you still mad at me? I did tell the truth. I just went up front because I wanted a rose for Mama. And you told me that I couldn't pick any, so are you mad?"

"No, " sighed her Papa.

Renata's parents didn't want to frighten their small daughter too much. They wanted her to believe that the world was still a good place. But they also had to protect her from the terrible things that were happening. How were they going to keep her safe?

Renata wondered too. There were so many things she was not supposed to do. Her parents weren't happy when she did things she had always done before Hitler came to power. Maybe if her Mama didn't work, she wouldn't get into so much trouble. She hated when her parents were mad at her. She hated her mother working. She wanted her carefree Mama back. Renata thought wistfully of the days she had spent in the sewing room, listening to her Mama's stories and hearing her laughter. She remembered all the things that she had looked forward to. It was true, she loved her new kindergarten and having friends, but she had never gotten that huge cone filled with candy. And now, her mama couldn't even spend much time with her. She pleaded with her Mama not to work. But her mother explained that they needed the money for food and clothing.

One day, Renata remained at home because she had a sore throat and she missed her mother even more. Renata thought, if I could find a way to get money, Mama could stay home with me, but how? How can a little girl get money? I know! She remembered the beggar children that she had seen. I will become a little beggar girl. I will ask people for money!

The first day that she was well, Greta took her to school, but Renata never entered the building. As soon as Greta said goodbye, Renata hid and waited until all the children were inside. Holding a small box that she had taken from home, she approached pedestrians on the street.

"Could you please give me some money? We have no money for food," she begged as her eyes filled with tears.

Quite a few people felt sorry for the small begging child and dropped some coins into the box. She continued begging for a few days.

No one at the school missed her since they assumed that she was still ill.

Every afternoon, when she returned home with Greta, she would hide the money under her bed. When the end of the week came, Renata proudly said to her mother, "Mama, you don't have to work anymore. We are rich now."

"What do you mean?" her mother asked absently, as she busied herself preparing dinner.

Renata ran and brought out the box filled with coins.

Her mother stared and sternly said, "Where did you get that money?"

"I was a little beggar girl and people gave it to me."

Her parents looked white with fear.

"Renata, don't you realize what might have happened if the German police saw you? You could be arrested. We might never see you again. Please Rena, I know that you want to be helpful and I know you love me, but we want to keep you safe. Please don't do anything without asking us first," her mother pleaded.

Turning to Greta, her father said, "Please watch her very, very carefully. You can never tell what she will think of next."

"I realize that now. I will be extremely careful."

So, Renata went to school every day and the months passed.

One day in June, Renata's Papa said, "We are going home to Offenburg. France has surrendered and the danger from the bombing is over."

Strangely enough, thought Renata, Papa doesn't sound very happy about it. "Papa, then we will see Oma and Opa again. Why aren't you happy?"

"Oh, little Renamaus," he sighed, "Hitler is stronger than ever, but," he added to make his child feel better, "don't you worry, things will get better. They must!"

So off to Offenburg they went.

CHAPTER 6

DEPORTATION

"Oma, Opa," yelled Renata excitedly, "we're home, we're home!"

Oma and Opa hugged their small granddaughters and showered them with kisses. "We missed you so." But, behind their smiles, Renata could sense that there was something wrong.

"What's the matter? Aren't you glad we're home?"

"Of course we are. Now don't worry about anything."

Renata hadn't been worried until that statement. But, not wanting to think about unhappy things, she quickly put it out of her mind.

"And you know what? Papa said that I could go to school in Freiburg now. I can go on the train with Eva and Miriam Cohen. And I'm going to stay all week with Aunt Lydia and Uncle Friederich and cousin Trude. Miriam and Eva will take care of me on the train, but I am really big enough to go by myself!"

"Well," said Oma, "you are excited. It all sounds wonderful. But, Rena, you are not big enough to go by yourself. You are to obey and listen to Miriam and Eva."

Mama sternly agreed.

When Renata left the room, Oma said to her daughter, "Do you think it's safe to let Rena go? She's always so talkative, even to strangers. And these days, Jews shouldn't be calling attention to themselves."

Ruth Haberer looked worried. "I know, but Rena must get an education. Besides, it is good for her to be in a classroom. There aren't any children her age left in Offenburg. I'll try to impress upon her the need to be careful."

Before Renata left on that first Sunday, her Mama spoke seriously to her. "Renata, when you are on the train, I don't want you to speak to any strangers. You are to listen carefully to Miriam and Eva. They are older, and are going to take care of you. You must obey them, as you do me."

"I will, Mama." Renata could hardly contain her excitement. "I will miss you. I won't see you for five whole days," she said sadly, but quickly her spirits rose. "But Mama, I do love trains!"

Renata took her little suitcase, filled it with her clothes for the week and stuck in Albert, her teddy bear. She thought she was probably too old to need her teddy bear, but she couldn't stand to be without him for almost a week.

She got on the train with every intention of listening to the older girls.

"Can I sit near the window?"

"Okay, but be quiet," Miriam answered, looking around anxiously. Luckily, the passengers didn't seem to be taking any notice of them.

For a few minutes Renata sat silently, gazing out of the window. Without thinking, she started to sing softly.

"Please be quiet," said Miriam, "we want to read. Besides, you'll draw attention to yourself."

"I'm only singing," said Renata. And Renata, still

unaware of the need to be silent, continued her song.

"If you sing, we'll sit somewhere else."

"That's okay," replied Renata. And the two girls moved to a seat further away, but where they could still keep an eye on her.

At the next station, a woman got on and took the vacant seat next to Renata. Renata smiled at her.

"Would you like a piece of candy?" the woman kindly asked.

"Yes thank you," answered Renata in her usual friendly way. And she started to chat with her seatmate.

At Freiburg, the girls got Renata and took her off the train.

"You know that you're not supposed to talk to anyone. We are going to tell your mother. You have to listen to us. This is no joke, Renata."

"I just forgot. I'll listen next time."

Renata's uncle met her at the train station, and took her to his house. Renata enjoyed being at her aunt and uncle's house. Since they had no young children, they tended to baby her. Also, she really enjoyed going to school. Unlike Offenburg, there were many children her own age, with whom she became friendly. When Friday came, she was happy to return to Offenburg to see her parents, and tell them about her new adventures.

"Now remember," said Miriam as they waited for the train, "no talking to anyone."

"Okay," and for the first fifteen minutes, she really tried. Then, restless sitting still, she decided to walk around the train. She smiled at the other passengers and when offered a cookie by one lady, she started talking. The two older girls sat nervously, hoping that Renata would not say anything that might get them in trouble. When they reached the Offenburg station, Miriam took her hand and helped her down.

"Frau Haberer, Renata keeps talking to strangers, even though you told her not to. She just won't listen to us."

"Is that true?" her Mama demanded.

"Mama, you know that you always told me that I had to be polite and answer people who spoke to me. Well, these people spoke to me first. So, I had to answer, didn't I?"

"I want you to be very quiet and sit still on the train. It is only a half hour. Please tell me I can trust you."

"I'll try," she sighed.

And she meant to. But every week, the same thing happened. Luckily, no one complained, and the girls remained safe.

Renata had been reading since she was three and could read almost anything. When Herr Kaufman, her teacher, discovered this, he said, "Renata I would like you to read an article from the newspaper to the class."

Suddenly Renata, who was rarely afraid of anything, felt shy. She shook her head worriedly. "What if I make a mistake?"

"That would be okay. We all make mistakes sometimes and I will be very proud of you for trying."

October 22, 1940—what a happy day this was going to be! Renata had practiced reading an article at home, thinking happily how proud her teacher would be of her. Ready for the big event, folding the newspaper in her rucksack, she went to school.

At ten o'clock, someone came to the classroom door. "Herr Kaufman, the school is being closed immediately. All Jewish schools in Baden-Württemberg have been ordered closed by the Nazis. The Jews are being rounded up. We must get the children home to their parents as soon as possible."

The teacher paled.

"Children, you are going home right now. Quickly, get your coats and rucksacks, and line up."

"But I haven't read yet and you won't be proud of me."

"I'm sorry," said Herr Kaufman. "Sometime soon, I hope," he added quietly.

Renata went to her aunt's house, where she found her suitcase already packed.

"Why am I going home, Aunt Lydia? I never even read the newspaper, and I practiced so hard."

Her aunt was very worried and hardly answered. "We can't talk now. I am going to put you on the train. You must get to your parents quickly. Don't say a word to anyone. Promise me."

Her aunt seemed so worried that Renata agreed that she would be absolutely still. For a minute she was frightened, but the thought of riding the train all by herself was very exciting. She felt extremely grown up when her aunt put her on the train. She sat by the window, feeling too much like an adult to wander around.

When she reached Offenburg, she got off the train and was startled that her parents were not there to meet her. Not her Mama, not her Papa, not Oma or Opa—where was everyone?

"Rena," she heard, and there was Herr Kramer, their upstairs neighbor. "All the Jewish people are going on a long trip. I'm going to bring you to the Turnhalle Gymnasium, where your Mama and Papa are."

"But if I'm going on a long trip, I have to get my things, and pack them," she told Herr Kramer.

"Your Mama packed all your things already."

"What about my princess bed? I need that."

"I will take care of it for you," he answered softly. "You know Frau Kramer and I love you."

The Kramers did love their young Jewish neighbor. It

was a brave thing for Herr Kramer to meet her at the station. German citizens were not supposed to be friends with the Jews. But Herr Kramer did not want Renata to be met by soldiers, and taken to her parents. Renata would be very frightened by that.

They walked the few blocks to the gymnasium, which was surrounded by soldiers. Herr Kramer took the little girl to the door.

"Here Rena, here is a bag of the raspberry candies that you like so much. Your parents are inside." He bent down and kissed her. He made the sign of the cross and quietly said, "God keep you safe." Quickly he turned and left.

"Inside!" a German soldier yelled. Renata moved toward the door. The huge hall was filled with people. All she could see were legs and more legs. There was so much shouting by the soldiers. Where was her Papa? Where was her Mama? How could she find them?

All at once, she heard her Papa's voice. "Here Renamaus, here." And there was her tall Papa reaching for her. He pulled her close and kissed her.

"Papa, what is happening?"

"I really don't know, but we are together, and that's what is important."

Rena nodded her head in agreement. And her Papa took her to the place where her Mama and Ellen, her grandparents and aunt and uncle from Friesenheim were gathered. Their suitcases were with them, and Renata sat down on one of them.

"Don't be scared, *Liebchen* (sweetheart)."

"I'm not now, because I am with you, Mama. I'm never scared when I'm with you. I always feel safe." She sat close to her mother.

Her mother half whispered to herself, "I hope that I can always keep you safe, my little one."

"Mama, I was supposed to read the newspaper to my class today. And then, they closed the school. But I did get to ride the train by myself. That was great. So I guess it's okay."

"I'll tell you what we'll do. You read the paper to Papa, Ellen and me, to Oma and Opa, and Aunt Brumhilde and Uncle Alfred. How would that be?"

"That's almost as good," said Renata.

"After you finish, I'll give you a cookie. Will that make you happy?"

"Okay," sighed Renata, and then she read the article as carefully as she could. She couldn't have had a more attentive and admiring audience. When she was done, everyone applauded and told her what a smart and wonderful girl she was. She ate her cookie and started to look about the hall, greeting people that were close by. All the people from Offenburg, and indeed, the whole area surrounding Offenburg were there. At least two thousand people were in the large hall. The rest of the day passed happily for the friendly little girl.

Towards nightfall, the gymnasium fell silent as a loud voice told everyone to gather their things. They were going to walk to the train station.

"Another train ride?" asked Renata. The worried expressions on the adult's faces should have warned her that this was not an exciting adventure. But all she heard was that they were going on a long train ride.

CHAPTER 7

THE TRAIN RIDE

Slowly, the hall that was filled with the Jews emptied, and the walk to the train began. Adults carried their luggage and tiny babies. Most small children needed to walk, as there were not enough arms to carry them. Renata carried her own little bag. Her mother had packed some food for the journey. When the soldiers had come to issue the deportation order, Frau Haberer had just cooked 10 pounds of potatoes to make potato salad. She decided to pack those potatoes with her luggage. It was those potatoes that kept the family from starving over the next few days.

When the Jews reached the Offenburg station, they were crowded into the train. Each railway car was divided into sections called coupes. Normally, each coupe held eight passengers. Renata's family of four, her grandparents and aunt and uncle and three others, eleven people in all, with their luggage, were crowded into one section. The Haberer family was one of the lucky ones. Many people were simply forced to stay in the aisles. Every inch of the train was jammed with people. Each car in the long train was packed. Six thousand Jews were being expelled from their native land. Slowly the train started to move.

Renata's father and uncle leaned against the window to see which direction the train was taking them. With anxious faces, they looked and looked, and finally Herr Haberer turned to his family, "*Shema Yisrael*, we are going west to France."

Everyone except Renata and Ellen knew what that meant. If they had been traveling east, it would have meant Polish camps, which were rumored to be death camps. Going west offered a ray of hope for their survival.

A long and interminable ride began. Crowded in the car, most fell asleep from exhaustion. Daylight awakened them from their uneasy slumber. Ruth Haberer gave everyone a small potato for breakfast.

"We'd best be careful with our food. We don't know how long we'll only have these potatoes to eat. We'll also have to share with those who have nothing."

Renata was restless. Oma entertained her with her wonderful stories. She and Oma sang their favorite songs but inevitably, Renata wanted to move about and see what was happening in the train.

"Mama, can I go visit the other coupes and see who I know?"

Her Papa said, "I want to see who is here, too. Renata can come with me."

They walked together and saw many people that they knew. Renata started to enjoy herself. She didn't understand why the adults weren't having fun.

So the first day passed—potatoes for breakfast, potatoes for lunch, potatoes for dinner. Trying to distract Rena and Ellen, the family members told stories, played games and sang songs. This helped to pass the time for them, as well as the small children. But oftentimes their thoughts about their future distracted them. Where were they being taken? What was going to happen? Were they going to be able to stay together?

A second day passed. They finished almost all the potatoes. There would be no other food once the potatoes were gone. They did not know if other food would be provided. Crowded in the car, they couldn't really sleep. Days and nights seemed longer and longer.

As the train headed west, picking up more Jews along the way, Papa and Renata would search for any family members that might have boarded the train. They discovered her aunt, uncle and cousin from Freiburg. Freiburg had been another major gathering place for the Jews of the area.

The third day dawned. The train stopped at Cannes, France. Some of the Jews of Cannes, hearing about the plight of their compatriots, unselfishly brought whatever food they could spare. All through the train, the Jews were generously sharing the food. One friend, who received some liver sausage, recalled that this was one of Renata's favorite foods and gave it to her. Still the train went on. The fifth day, Quakers, a religious group, and the Red Cross brought food. Although the supply was minimal, it did save many passengers from starvation. For seven days, the Jewish people remained on the train.

When the Jews were deported from Germany, Gauleiter Wagoner, who was in charge of the upper Rhineland region, wanted to make the Baden-Württemberg area *Judenfrei* (free of Jews), but he couldn't bring himself to send people to the German-occupied camps in Poland. So he contacted Vichy France and asked them to grant the Jews from his area asylum. They agreed. The Quakers, the Red Cross and the *Oeuvre de Secours aux Enfants* (Society for Rescuing Children), better know as the OSE, looked for a place to put the refugees. They kept them on the train, while they searched for a location to accommodate 6,000 Jews. Finally, they decided to take them to Le Camp de Gurs.

The evening before the transfer to Gurs, an internment camp, German officers decided to collect whatever money the Jews had with them. When the order for the deportation came, the Jews were told they could bring one suitcase and up to 50 marks per person. This was equivalent to about $100 U.S. Now, the officers informed the Jews that they had to pay for the train ride!

The soldiers collected the money from Renata's coupe first, and told her father to come with them to help collect the rest of the money from the other passengers.

Most people, knowing that they were powerless, surrendered their money. But when the officers entered one compartment, an elderly lady refused. She had hidden her money in her undergarments.

"*Nein* (No)," she said. "I can keep my money. The orders said 50 marks a person."

The soldier was furious. "How dare you argue with a soldier of the Third Reich," he roared, and pushed the old woman with his rifle, knocking her to the floor.

Renata's caring and courageous father could bear no more. Not having learned his lesson at Dachau, he reached out and shoved the soldier across the coupe!

Immediately the other soldiers grabbed him and threw him out of the car and put him into solitary confinement. They guarded him with their rifles raised.

Passengers who saw this unfold, wondered what would happen. Renata's family quickly learned what had occurred. They were terrified. Would their beloved Gustel be shot? All night they waited in fear.

In the morning, the train was emptied. Families were separated; women and children were loaded on to some trucks while men were put on others. Still no word of Gustel! Finally, he was marched out of the train. The captain in charge stared at him.

"Don't ever do anything like that again. You are a Jew! You have no rights! You are no longer a free citizen of Germany," but surprisingly, he didn't shoot Herr Haberer. He knew that because he was a Jew, he would never survive. He let him board one of the trucks.

Though they didn't know it then, this act of courage and humanity helped save the Haberer family.

CHAPTER 8

LE CAMP DE GURS

When the trucks entered Le Camp de Gurs, the gates closed behind them.

"Mama," asked Renata, "What are those wires all around?"

"That's barbed wire, Rena. You must never touch it. It can cut you badly."

"But Mama, why are we locked in? Mama this is like a jail. Why are we in jail? We didn't do anything."

"Remember what I told you honey, the Jews didn't do anything bad. You must never feel that we did. Some bad people are in power now. But they will be punished one day. Rena, it will be okay."

Rena let herself be comforted by her mother's words. She thought that she could always trust her Mama. With her fear gone, Renata looked around. All she could see were old crumbling shacks that she later learned were called barracks. They were blackened by weather and were set in a sea of mud. Mud, black and slick, was everywhere. She had never seen such mud!

The camp was divided into sections called *Ilots* (small island). Each *Ilot* had twenty-two to twenty-four barracks, surrounded by barbed wire. Each section was guarded, as you were not permitted to go from one *Ilot* to another. The men were sent to *Ilots* at one end of the camp while the women and children were sent to the other. Renata, her mother, and Ellen were sent to *Ilot* M. Her aunts were with them, but sadly, her Oma was put in *Ilot* L. They could see each other through the barbed wire but were not able to touch.

Renata entered her barracks with about fifty other people. It was completely bare. There were no tables or chairs, no beds, just straw configured into beds on the earthen ground.

Living conditions were terrible. The shacks were filthy. They were rife with rats and other vermin. At night, the rats would come out and bite anyone who was sleeping.

Renata's Mama sat up all night cradling Ellen in her arms while Renata slept across her lap. Her aunts took turns throwing shoes to keep the rats away. The women were always exhausted.

There were no bathrooms. A pump with cold water was outside. People washed under the pump. When it turned very cold, Renata's mother sponge-bathed the children in the barracks, which did not provide much more warmth than being outside. Worse were the toilets. They were just big holes surrounded by wood, with no privacy. It was smelly and disgusting. Renata refused to use them. She was afraid that she might fall into the huge hole. She was becoming very sick, until her mother convinced her that she had to be very brave and use those holes. Mama assured her that she would be there to hold her tightly.

Worst of all, there was nothing to do. Renata wandered around, in her boots, on the slippery mud. She learned to lean forward to keep her balance. Whenever it rained, and it rained often, the mud would be so deep and slippery that the only way that she could walk was to hold the hand of an adult. The only good thing about Gurs, as opposed to other camps, was that the guards were French and not German. The French did not hate the Jews as much as the Germans did.

The *Ilot* that her family was in bordered a cemetery. It was there that Renata went every day. She would stand at the barbed wire separating the *Ilot* from the cemetery and watch the constant funeral processions. Eight hundred Jews died that first winter. Relatives were allowed to bury their loved ones, and they wept as they walked to the burial grounds. Renata also wept as she watched. She wasn't crying for the unknown people. She was just so unhappy, and the funerals gave her the excuse to shed her tears.

One day she noticed a guard at the barbed wire. He reminded her of her Papa, as he was tall and had dark hair. She just had to talk to him.

"Hello," she said shyly.

The guard ignored her. That didn't stop Renata. Everyday, she greeted him. And everyday, he ignored her.

One morning, when Renata was standing in the deep dark mud, the guard accidentally dropped his glove under the barbed wire. Before it could sink deeper in the mud, Renata crawled under the wire and picked up the filthy glove. She gave him a big smile as she handed it to him.

The guard could no longer ignore her. This guard knew how to speak a little German as his mother had come from the Alsace region of France, where German was spoken.

"*Danke* (Thank you). What is your name?"

"Renata."

"Why do you come here everyday?"

"There is nothing else to do."

Going to the cemetery became happier for Renata. She and the guard would talk of many things. Renata would tell him how much she missed her Papa.

"Mama, come meet my guard. He is a very nice man," she would often say when she would return to the barracks.

"No, Renata, I don't want to meet any guards. I wish that you wouldn't either."

"But then I wouldn't have anything to do," and she continued with her daily trips to the cemetery.

One day the guard said, "Renata, if you could go to see your Papa, would you be afraid to walk all by yourself all the way to the other side of the camp?"

"No, I want to see my Papa. I miss him so much and I am never afraid."

"Ask your Mama to come and see me, and if she agrees, I think that I can arrange for you to visit your Papa."

Renata plodded back through the mud as quickly as she could.

"Mama, Mama," she called.

"What is it Rena?"

"Mama," she said breathlessly, "my guard wants you to come to see him and talk to him."

"Does he really want to talk to me or did you say my Mama wants to talk to you?"

"No, he said so. He really did. He said to come tomorrow morning."

Renata's mother agreed, wondering what had happened. She was worried because guards did not usually ask to see a prisoner unless something was wrong.

The following morning, she went with Renata to the barbed wire near the cemetery. She looked apprehensively at the guard standing there.

The guard said, "Renata has told me how much she

wants to see her Papa. I have talked to the other guards in the *Ilots* between this one and the one where your husband is. They have agreed to allow the child through, if you give your permission."

"I thought that no visits were allowed."

"It's been decided to permit visitation between the men's and women's *Ilots*. It will be started shortly. That is why I was able to arrange for Renata's visit."

"Is it safe for her to go alone?"

"We will watch her carefully. She will be able to walk on the wooden sidewalk."

"Renata," asked her mother, "will you be afraid to go by yourself?'

"Oh no, Mama, please let me go."

Frau Haberer reluctantly gave her permission.

The visit was arranged for the next day.

"That's quite a little girl you have there," the guard said.

The next morning, Renata set out on her journey. She was loaded with letters from the women in her barracks to their husbands, fathers, sons, brothers, and friends. Women had bartered goods for some food, which they also sent.

Renata, feeling very brave and important, started her long walk. As she passed each *Ilot*, the people waved and she happily smiled and waved back. She felt like a queen. It really was a great adventure!

Finally, she reached her Papa's *Ilot*. He had been informed that his daughter was coming and was awaiting her arrival anxiously.

"Renamaus," he called when he saw her. He held out his arms and she flew into them. Tears filled his eyes as he hugged his little girl.

"Papa, I am so happy to see you. I miss you so much."

"Me too, my little Renamaus. Tell me, how are Mama and Ellen?"

"Papa, I have a letter for you from Mama. It will tell you everything. And I have letters for Opa and a lot of other people too."

"Let me read my letter while you deliver all your mail."

As Renata delivered her letters and food, she talked to the people she knew. She noticed how changed they were. Her Uncle Alfred, who always had a huge stomach, was now thin. None of the men looked as she remembered. All were very skinny.

However, she soon forgot this as they greeted her warmly. They hadn't seen a child in such a long time. One man had gotten hold of a banana, which he gave to Renata. She felt wonderful with all the attention that she received. Best of all, was being with her wonderful Papa and Opa.

All too soon, the time she was allotted grew to a close. The men gave her letters for their wives and relatives. Her Papa gave her one last kiss and hug, and off she went on her long way back. Renata would gladly have made the trip every day. But, alas, no more permission was granted.

Renata had another idea. When she came to the cemetery's barbed wire again, she said to the guard, "Somebody died in my barracks, now there is room for another person and I really want my Oma to come. Could I speak to the man in her *Ilot* to see if he will let her?"

"You want to see the man in charge? Is that what you want?" The guard was amused. "Do you mean a guard like me?"

"Could *you* let her come?"

"No, I'm afraid not."

"Then I don't want to speak to you. I want to speak to the man who could."

Entertained by the audacity of her request, the guard decided to speak to the officer in charge. When the commanding officer heard that a little girl of seven wanted to speak to him, he also was quite amused, and agreed to see her.

When Renata arrived, she curtsied before the officer.

"Why do you want to see me?"

"Its about my Oma. She's in your *Ilot* and I miss her so much. There is room in my barracks because a lady died. So can my Oma come to live with me?"

"What's your Oma's name?"

"Tilla Strauss."

"Why is it so important to you?"

"She tells me stories and sings with me and I just love her so very much."

The man thought for a moment. He knew what was being planned for the Jews in the camp. And the future was not going to be a happy one for the little girl. Why shouldn't he do what he could, to make her happy now?

"Any Oma who has such a brave little granddaughter deserves to be with her. I will transfer her to your *Ilot*."

"Thank you, oh, thank you so much!"

He smiled and told the guard to tell Tilla Strauss to pack her things and come to the commander's office.

When Frau Strauss heard the order, she was very frightened. She didn't know where she was being sent. Was it to another camp? Was it one of the terrible camps that were being whispered about?

She entered the office. When Renata saw her with her suitcase, she ran and kissed her. Then she quickly ran across the room, threw her arms around the commanding officer and said, "You are the nicest man in the whole, wide world."

And now, Renata had her adored Oma, whose love and laughter helped her forget the dreadful hardship of the Camp de Gurs.

CHAPTER 9

GUSTEL HABERER

Visitation between the men and women of the camp was now permitted. Renata's father, Gustel, came to visit Ruth's *Ilot.*

After a joyful reunion with his wife, children, sisters and mother-in-law, he said to his wife, "Ruth, come walk with me for a while. I have a lot to tell you."

As they walked outside the barracks, where they couldn't be overheard, he told her what had happened since he had last seen her. When he and the other men had been brought to the camp, he had been appalled by the filthy conditions of the place. He also noted the lethargy settling on the men and felt that he had to do something, anything to get them involved. He asked to see the commander of his *Ilot* and then he requested permission to establish a work detail to clean up the place. All he wanted were some cleaning tools to work with.

"Why do you want to do this?" the commander asked. "I can't give you more food. I don't have it. I can't give you anything. Well, maybe, I could get a little more food, just for you, but certainly for no one else."

"No, I'm not asking for extra privileges," Gustel answered firmly.

"Then why, why should you do this?"

"First, to just clean the place, so that we aren't living in such filth. But also, I want to give the men a reason to get up in the morning, to be tired when night comes, to simply have something to do."

"Very well, I'll give you what you asked for, but nothing more. Don't ask for anything else."

"Thank you, that's all I want."

Gustel Haberer organized the men. At first, only some volunteered. But, eventually all the men cooperated in cleaning their *Ilot.*

The French Underground heard of Gustel's work, and further, how he had bravely stood up to the German soldier on the train. They realized Gustel was a man of strong character and courage, so they had one of their members secretly approach him.

The French Underground was a secret army. It was made up of men and women who performed daring deeds and sabotage to help defeat the Germans. They dynamited railway tracks and bridges to prevent supplies from getting through to the German army. They helped political prisoners escape from concentration camps. It was exceedingly dangerous work. And if a member was caught, he was tortured and killed. As a result, only very brave people worked for the French Underground.

Seeking out Gustel Haberer, they asked if he would be willing to help them.

"I would do anything in my power to defeat Hitler and the Nazis. How am I able to help?"

"We need someone to help several political prisoners escape."

"How could I do that?"

"We would get you a job in the soup kitchen which is being set up by the Quakers and the Red Cross. Every day, the huge pots will be wheeled outside the camp to be washed. At certain times, you will be asked to hide a prisoner in one of these pots and wheel him outside the camp. If you are caught, we won't be able to help you. You know what that means."

Ruth held him close when she heard this. "It is so dangerous."

"I must do it. I must do all I can to stop this madness. I can't simply sit back and let others do the fighting. I have to do whatever I can to fight for what I believe in."

"Oh Gustel, I know, but I am so frightened."

"You want to see us free?"

"Yes, of course, just be careful. I love you and I am so very proud of you."

The days went by. Renata had her eighth birthday in Gurs. Meanwhile, the *Oeuvre de Secours aux Enfants* (OSE) was working to free the Jewish children. In the interim, they were given permission to organize schools for the young people in the camp. Special barracks were set up and more food was to be given to the children. These barracks were warmer and cleaner, and Renata was to be sent there.

She was not happy. "Why do I have to go, Mama? I like being with you and Oma. I don't want to go to another barracks and school."

"Rena, education is very important. It is the job of every child to go to school. You must be educated. It is one of the things that Papa and I want most for you and Ellen. And Rena, you will still be near me. You'll still see me everyday. It won't be as bad as when you went to Freiburg."

"But, Mama—"

"No buts, you will go to school."

Renata had been in Gurs for four months. She was going to school and she expected her life to continue in this way. One day her father came to speak to his wife.

"Ruth, the OSE has arranged for some children to leave the camp and go to a children's home in unoccupied France. It is only for children ten and older—but do you remember Madame Salomon from the children's home where we worked at in Munich? Well, through her connections, we are able to send Rena, even though she's only eight."

"How can I let her go? She is so young. She needs me and—I need her too."

"It may be the only way we can save her. I wish Ellen could go, but right now, they do not have any facilities for little ones."

Ruth paled. "Are things as bad as that?"

"Germany continues to conquer the countries of Europe, and there are rumors that we are to be sent elsewhere—places that will make this camp look like a resort. Awful things are happening Ruth. I hate to tell you this, but you must understand the necessity of sending Rena away. Hitler means to rid Europe of all the Jews. And we have to do everything possible to save our children."

"I know it must be done, but how can I tell her? She keeps saying everything is okay if she is with me. When are they supposed to be going?"

"In just a few days. The plans are all made. We just have to sign the necessary papers."

Ruth did not tell her daughter until the day before she was supposed to leave. She wanted to keep her happy as long as possible. The few days sped by.

CHAPTER 10

A SAD FAREWELL

"Rena, come sit with me. I have something to tell you," her mother called.

"Mama, you look so sad."

"I am, darling. This will be hard for you and even harder for me, but it is for the best."

"What?"

Renata was scared.

"The OSE has arranged for you and some of the other children to go to a children's home in unoccupied France."

"No, Mama, no! I don't want to leave you. Don't make me, Mama. I'll be good. I'll do everything you tell me. I'll go to school. I'll eat the terrible soup. I'll do everything you want."

"Rena, I'm not sending you because you aren't good. You are a wonderful daughter. You're my brave little girl. I am doing this because I love you so much. You will sleep in a real bed. You won't have to worry about rats. You will have a real bathroom, but most of all, you will be safe. It will be much better. It really will."

"It's only better when I'm with you."

"Renata, Papa and I know what is best for you. Even if you don't understand, you just have to accept that."

"But, Ellen will still be with you."

"I wish she could go too, but they are not taking any children under ten. Papa was lucky to get special permission for you, although you are only eight."

"Please, Mama, wait until I am ten. I will be so lonely. I need you."

"I'll write to you, and Renata, you never have to be lonely. It's going to be very hard for you and for me when you leave, but you will never be alone. All you have to do is close your eyes, and you will see Papa and me and all the people you love. We will always be with you. And now," she said, changing the subject, "I am going to make you two new skirts to take with you."

For a moment, Renata was distracted. "How will you do that? You have no material or sewing machine."

"But, I have needles and thread and scissors. I am going to cut up two of my skirts for you. Come, sit near me like you used to do in the sewing room and we will talk as I sew. There are some things I want you to always remember. First, I've told you this before, but I will say it again because it is so important. Don't ever be ashamed of being Jewish. What is happening is not a punishment from God. The Jewish people have done nothing wrong. There are some terrible people like Hitler who are in power right now, and they are doing these things to us. Those people should be ashamed for what they are doing. But it will change and things will get better. The good Lord will punish those people. It will take a while, but it will happen."

"Let me stay with you, Mama. You know it will get better. You said so."

"But, Rena, I don't know when," she sighed. "And whatever happens, I want you to be safe."

Ruth Haberer thought about what words she could give her little daughter to help her through these terrible times. How could she help her grow into the kind of person that she wanted her to be? So young, so very young to be going out on her own.

"Renata you will have to think for yourself. Papa and I won't be with you to get you out of trouble. Think before you act. Promise me, darling, you will always try to be careful."

Renata nodded her head. She would try.

"Good. Now, when you go away, you might be taken to church. If you are, you are to go there happily. You never have to feel you are doing anything wrong. It doesn't make any difference if you are in a church or a synagogue. The building belongs to the Lord and not to the people. In God's house there are no strangers, so you go and you pray because you are praying to God and He will listen."

What else should I tell her, Renata's mother wondered. There is so much she will need to know, and I won't be there to help her. What did I want to know when I was her age?

"Rena, when you are older you will want to know where babies come from." She thought what can I tell her that she will understand now, and yet, will help her in the future. "Children," she continued, "are born because when two people love each other very much, they want to have something that is a part of each of them, so the good lord created a miracle. That miracle allows two people who love each other very much, to create a child."

"Is that why Papa and you had Ellen and me?"

"Yes, *liebchen*, and always remember how much we love you, and how very proud we are of you." Her mother held her close and kissed her. Ruth's eyes filled with tears at the thought of her child growing up without her.

"Now close your eyes and sleep. I'll hold you on my lap until morning." Renata didn't want to sleep. She didn't want morning to ever come. But, inevitably, the hours moved on and morning dawned.

CHAPTER 11

ASPET

The transport of the children began. Carrying small pieces of luggage, they clung to their mothers and cried as they were asked to board the trucks that were to take them to the train station. Trains no longer held any enchantment for Renata.

Two mothers were permitted to accompany the children on the trip to the station. And since Renata was the youngest child going, her mother was one of the two chosen. Renata did not cry on the truck. Her Mama was with her, and she could still hope they wouldn't be separated. However, when the truck reached the station, and Renata realized her Mama was actually leaving, she wrapped her arms around her, and clutched onto her with all her might.

"Mama, Mama," she sobbed, "don't make me go. Please, please!"

Her mother couldn't speak. She was choked up with her own tears. How could she tear her own child from her body? She couldn't—but she had to. She had to!

Suddenly Madame Andree Salamon appeared. She was a

wonderful woman who was spending all of her time and energy trying to save the Jewish children. Seeing what was happening, and knowing what had to be done, she scooped Renata up in her arms and placed her on a seat on the train. Renata just sat there. On the whole trip, she sat rigidly while the tears silently streamed down her face.

The sadness that coursed though her entire body never left her. Eventually, in the days ahead, the tears would stop, but the deep misery remained. Renata's spirit seemed to have disappeared.

The train reached Toulouse, and the children were transferred to a truck headed to The Children's Home in Aspet. It was located just outside the city.

For a while, on the train, the older children tried to cheer Renata, but they too, were unhappy. Her withdrawn quietness and misery made their loneliness more acute, and their reaction, unfortunately, was to tease her. She withdrew even further.

The attitudes on all their parts were additionally aggravated by the first night's events. When they went to bed that evening, Renata lay longing for her Mama. Secretly, feeling she was too old to sleep with her teddy bear, but needing to hold something she loved, she removed Albert from her suitcase. He was old now; his arms and legs were gone, but she still loved him. It was a bit of home. She also took out the brown wool skirt that her Mama had made her. Holding the two items in her arms, she fell into a restless sleep. Towards morning, she dreamt she went to the bathroom and for the first time since she was a baby, she wet the bed. Renata woke with a start. She had to examine the sheet, and when she pulled back the cover, one of the girls in the dormitory noticed the wet spot.

"Look," she cried to the others in the room, "Look at

the big baby."

"Baby, baby," taunted another, "and she even sleeps with a teddy bear."

"A beat up teddy bear, too. What a baby!"

It went on for what seemed like hours. But in reality, it was only a few moments. Renata never said a word. She lay down on the bed again, with her eyes closed, pretending not to hear.

Mademoiselle Resch, who was in charge of Renata's group, heard the shrieks and high-pitched laughter. She ran into the dormitory. Seeing what was happening, she said, "You girls should be ashamed of yourselves. I'm surprised at your cruelty."

Embarrassed, the girls moved away and Renata, with Mademoiselle Resch's help, changed the sheets and her clothes.

Renata remained in Aspet for over a year, from February 1941 to March 1942. In all that time, she never forgave the girls. For the first time in her life, she was spiritless and friendless.

CHAPTER 12

ON TO LIMOGES

During the first few months at Aspet, Renata received mail from her parents, grandparents, aunts and uncles. Then silence. What had happened?

She wondered, who was she? Was she French or German? Did she have a family? Was there a place for her?

She was so miserable that it was an effort to get out of bed in the morning, to wash, to dress, to eat. The only respite was school. She was a good student and the work forced her to think about something besides her own unhappiness. She was learning French and could soon speak it as if it was her native tongue. But the rest of the time, she lived in her own sad world.

Madame Salomon, the representative of the OSE, came to see her.

"Renata, the reason you haven't heard from your parents is that they have been transferred to Rivesaltes, another camp. They were not allowed to send letters while they were being transferred."

"Are my Mama and Papa alright?" she asked anxiously.

"Yes, they are."

Renata breathed easier. "What about Oma and Opa and everyone else?"

"Your Oma and aunts and uncles are all okay, too. They're all in Rivesaltes."

"What about my Opa?" she asked, noticing the omission.

"He was sent to Drancy, another camp. I am sorry, Renata, that's all I know. But now, I have some good news for you. Your sister Ellen is being sent to a children's home in Limoges. I know from Mademoiselle Resch that you haven't been happy here…"

Renata interrupted, "I hate it here!"

"Well, we can change that now. Your parents would like you and Ellen to be together, so we are going to send you to Limoges. Do you think you'd like that?"

"Oh yes, yes, any place but here. Besides, it will be wonderful to be with Ellen."

When she arrived at the Children's Home in Limoges, she was amazed when she saw Ellen. In the year she hadn't seen her sister, the three-year-old had changed greatly. Tall for her age, Ellen was almost as big as the tiny Renata. Beautiful as ever, she was no longer the baby Renata remembered, but a young child.

A year is a very long time when you are only three. She stood still and stared at Renata.

"Ellen, do you remember me? I'm Rena."

"I think so. Mama told me you'd be here."

Suddenly, Ellen's face crumpled. "I want Mama," she said, and burst into tears. Renata understood just how she felt. She also knew how her Mama would want her to act. She put her arms around her young sister, and held her tightly.

"Don't worry, Ellen. I'm here, and I'll take care of you. We'll be okay."

Later that day, Renata started to wonder. How come her parents had sent little Ellen to a children's home? She was only a baby. How come they were taking children who were only four? When she had been sent to Aspet, she had been eight and that was an exception. The other children had all been at least ten years of age, so what was happening now?

What Renata didn't know was how terrible conditions were at Rivesaltes. Gurs was awful, but the new camp was infinitely worse. Besides, Rivesaltes was a deportation camp. From there, the Jews were being sent to Auschwitz, Hitler's final solution. This was Hitler's culmination of his obsession to rid the world of Jews. Could such a thing happen in a civilized country in the twentieth century? If this was true, it was imperative to save as many children as possible, even if it meant separating babies from their mothers.

The war was going badly for the Allied countries. The United States, England, and other Allies were losing. Germany was conquering most of Europe, and the underground was doing all it could to help the Allies. Gustel Haberer was still working for them. He helped many political prisoners escape. The manner in which he accomplished this made the people in the underground like and respect him. When they discovered what was going to happen to the Jews in Rivesaltes, one of Gustel's contacts came to him with a proposition.

"If we can manage to find a way for you and your wife to escape, would you be willing to do demolition work for us? We will train you, but I must warn you that it is extremely dangerous work."

"I'll do anything in my power to defeat Hitler, but I want you to get my mother-in-law and sisters to safety, as well."

"No, I'm terribly sorry, but that's impossible. It will be

difficult enough to get you and your wife out. Have you any idea where the inmates in this camp are being sent?"

"I've heard rumors, but I can't leave my family. We've been through so much together; we'll continue to stay together. I have to take care of them, as much as I can. Perhaps, I will be able to save them."

"Think about this carefully, Gustel."

That afternoon, the commandant, who had previously been at Gurs, called Gustel to his quarters, ostensibly to fix something. Gustel was very handy, and the commandant had often used him in this capacity. He had grown to like this brave and bright man. Suddenly, without looking at Gustel, he said, "If anyone can get out of this place, he should."

Gustel became alert. "Are you telling me something?"

"Remember, you never heard this from me, but, if you have any chance to escape, do it."

"I can't just leave my sisters and mother-in-law."

"Where they are going, no one can help them. Remember, I said nothing! I'm trusting you, Gustel, not to repeat what I said to anyone."

"You can trust me. I appreciate what you are doing. But, what should I do?"

"Make your decision fast. There isn't much time."

Gustel thought and thought. How could he leave the others to this certain fate? He realized he also had Ellen and Renata to consider. If he left, not only would he be helping to win the war against Hitler, but there was a chance, he could be with his children again. They were so young to be left alone in the world.

When his contact returned for his answer, the man said, "We have found a way to get your mother-in-law out, but only if you know someone in Free France who will take her in. It is impossible for her to stay in the places you and your wife will be sent."

"I have cousins there. I know they will take her. Thank you for that. And yes," he sighed, "I will go, but I want you to send my wife to a place of safety."

"That can be arranged."

Ruth Haberer insisted on remaining with her husband and helping with the underground. The three of them were smuggled out of Rivesaltes, and given new names and identities. Gustel and Ruth were sent from place to place learning new skills. Gustel was taught how to do demolition work, and Ruth learned how to help in the preparation of false identification papers.

Not aware of all that was happening to her parents, Renata could think of no answer to her question. Why had they let Ellen go? Maybe they just wanted Ellen and me to be together. Knowing there was no way to find out the reason, she put it out of her mind. She was determined to help Ellen.

Not only did this attitude help her sister, but it helped Renata as well. Thinking of someone other than herself, trying to be cheerful for Ellen's sake, she became her old self. Her interest in people and surroundings returned. Although she still missed her parents, she made friends, was happy, high spirited, and a chatterbox as well.

One day, her insatiable desire to talk almost proved to be catastrophic. She was whispering to her friend in school, when her teacher said, "Renata, one more time and I'll send you out of the room."

Renata tried to be quiet, but suddenly remembered something she just had to say to her best friend. "Janine," she whispered…

"Renata," came her teacher's voice, "I've told you over and over again. Now wait outside until I can talk to you."

Renata walked slowly to the door of the classroom. Her

eyes welled up. I'm going to leave school right now, she thought. I'll tell Madame (the headmistress of The Children's Home) what happened before the teacher can talk to her. I'll think up a good excuse, and maybe then, she won't be terribly angry with me.

She started the long walk home from school. She had always walked to and from school with the other children. Renata came to a road that bordered a forest. She had never paid attention to the forest, since she was always distracted by her friends. Now it seemed dark and threatening.

Suddenly a group of German soldiers appeared. They were patrolling the area. The sergeant in charge stopped in front of Renata. "Where are you going?" he asked.

"I'm going home," she replied. Some awareness made her speak French.

"At this time? Why aren't you at school?"

Renata eyes filled. "I talked, and the teacher sent me out of the room. I didn't mean to be bad," and now she really wished that she held her tongue.

The soldier softened when he saw the tears. "I have a little girl like you at home. She also talks too much at times. Now, I want you to promise me never to do that again. Besides, the Easter Bunny won't bring you any candy if you're not a good girl."

Renata did not tell him that she was Jewish, and that an Easter Bunny would not come anyway. She simply hung her head and nodded. "I promise I'll never talk in school again."

"Remember that," said the sergeant. "Now we'll walk you to the edge of the forest, and then you run as fast as you can. It's dangerous for a little girl to be out here alone."

Renata did not have to be told twice. She ran as fast as she could to The Children's Home. She was no longer worried about a mere punishment. That was very unimportant now.

By the time she arrived home, her teacher had already called to inform the Madame that Renata had left the school. When she had found Renata missing, she had been panicky that the Germans had picked up the child. Often when this happened, the child was never seen again. Everyone at the home was frantic, so when Renata arrived, there was such a feeling of relief that she was safe, no one bothered to scold her about talking in class.

She was happy in Limoges. She enjoyed school; she had her friends and sister. Her only unhappiness was being separated from her parents and other members of her family. She had not seen her Mama or Papa for eighteen months. Eighteen months, a year and a half, is a long time for anyone, but at eight years of age it is an eternity. Renata wondered if it would ever end.

One day in October 1942, two months before her tenth birthday, one of the children excitedly came to Renata.

"Madame says that you are to go to the office. You have a visitor!"

"A visitor! Who is it? Do you know? Is it my Mama?"

"I don't know. Go on. You'll find out soon enough."

Renata ran to the office. When she opened the door, her heart fell. It wasn't her Mama. It wasn't even anyone she knew. It was only a very pretty young woman.

Renata made a polite little curtsey. Madame smiled.

"I have some good news for you, but first, I want you to meet Mademoiselle Nicole. She will give you the news."

Renata smiled and Nicole said, "Well Renata, I do have some good news. I'm going to take you and Ellen to visit your parents."

Renata ran to Nicole and grabbed her hand. "Really, truly? Am I going to stay with them?"

Nicole's face clouded. "No, I'm afraid not. It will be a short visit and then, I'm going to take you to Switzerland where you will be safe. Switzerland is a neutral country. That means they are not involved in the war, so the Germans can't hurt you there."

"But I don't want to go to Switzerland. I want to be with my Mama and Papa."

"I know how you feel about that, but these are unusual, terrible times. You can talk to your parents about it, but now, we have to hurry. We have to catch a train shortly, so we can get you to your parents today. All you will be able to carry is your little rucksack. Don't worry about your clothes, just take anything you feel you must have."

Renata thought for a moment. It is useless to try to convince Nicole, but I know that I can make my Mama and Papa let me stay with them. I know it—especially my Papa. I can always get my way with him. I'll think of some really good reasons and they won't be able to say no.

With that thought she ran to her room, and grabbed her rucksack. What did she really want? Albert—she couldn't leave her teddy bear. He had always been with her. I may be too old for a teddy bear, but I want him! I just can't leave him.

Albert, who had helped comfort her in Aspet and Limoges, and even further back in Munich and Freiburg, was still loved. Luckily, his lack of arms and legs allowed Renata to squeeze him into her rucksack. The only other thing she took was the brown wool skirt her mother had made for her that last night in Gurs. She decided to wear the blue skirt, the other one her mother had made.

Renata went to say goodbye to her friends.

"You're so lucky. You'll see your parents," her friend Lissy said. "Will you stay with them?"

"I will," Renata said firmly.

"How I wish that would happen to me," replied Lissy.

"It will. I know it will."

Happy for Renata, the other girls felt hopeful that they too would be reunited with their families.

The girls hugged and kissed, and blowing a last kiss, Renata returned to the office. Ellen was already there.

"Now," said Nicole "I have a big treat for you." She handed each of them a piece of chocolate. Renata was thrilled. She couldn't remember the last time she had chocolate. It must have been years! Certainly, it had been before they had been deported. She was just going to put it in her mouth when she had a better idea.

"Listen Ellen," she said, "let's save our chocolate and give it to Mama and Papa."

"Okay," the smaller girl answered, and they put the candy in Renata's rucksack. What a sacrifice for a girl who adored candy so much. But, Renata had something even more wonderful in store for her. She was going to see her Mama and Papa.

CHAPTER 13

ANOTHER FAREWELL

On the train, Renata, now almost ten, sat still, but five-year-old Ellen started to walk around. Suddenly the train lurched forward and Ellen fell, banging her head. She started to howl. Nicole looked at her anxiously.

"Renata, see if you can quiet her. We can't afford to call attention to ourselves."

Renata rushed over and helped Ellen up. "Stop crying, Ellen. Please be quiet," she begged.

Ellen continued to cry. "I'll tell you what," pleaded Renata, "if you're quiet you can eat your piece of chocolate and we'll give Mama and Papa mine to share."

At that, Ellen howled even louder. "I ate mine. I ate yours too! I took them out of your rucksack when you weren't looking and I ate them."

Now Renata could have howled too. "How could you? How could you be so mean?" Seeing her sister's face, she added, "Okay. I'll forgive you if you'll be quiet. Now come and sit beside me and I'll tell you a story."

Renata told her the story of Hansel and Gretel. She

remembered how much she had loved the fairy tale when she was her sister's age.

Presently, the train reached Brives, the town where their parents were temporarily housed. The three walked to the Haberers' quarters.

"Mama, Papa!" Renata hugged and kissed her parents. They held her and Ellen tight in their arms as if they'd never let them go. Ruth looked at her older daughter. "I can't believe how you've grown Rena," she said. "I'm still not very tall," Renata answered ruefully.

"But you're almost a young lady, nearly ten years old." And Renata had changed dramatically. Gone was the impetuous child. A more responsible young girl had taken her place. Pleased and proud, her mother wistfully missed the changes she had not been there to witness. "Oh, I can't believe we're together. And Ellen, you're five now, just the time to be starting school. I've missed you both so much. Now I want you to tell me everything that has happened to you."

Their Papa nodded in agreement. He couldn't take his eyes off his two daughters.

Renata began telling about her life for the last twenty months. She told her parents how unhappy she had been in Aspet, and how mean the girls had been to her.

"But you were happy in Limoges, weren't you?" asked her mother.

"Yes, everybody was nice there. I had lots of friends, and the Madame was very good to everyone, but I wasn't as happy as I am right now with you. Mama, Papa, can't we stay with you?"

"No Rena, it simply isn't possible. As much as we want you to, it's just too dangerous. The Germans are looking for you and Ellen. They learned that the man doing the demolition work here has two daughters in a Jewish

Children's home, and since they haven't been able to capture your Papa, they decided to search for you and Ellen. They know that your Papa would give himself up to save you. If Papa is worried about his two girls, he can't do his job well. And Rena, what he is doing is very important for all of us. That is why we are sending you to Switzerland."

"Look," reasoned Renata, "I can speak French now. Nobody knows I'm German, so I'll be a little French girl. The Germans will never know who I am. I'll be so good. I'll watch Ellen, and I won't let her say anything. Please, please don't send me away again. Please Mama."

"Renamaus," interrupted her father, "there is to be no argument. You must go to Switzerland. Now, I have some information for you. I'm going to tell you the names of some cousins we have in Switzerland. They live in the city of Zurich, and their names are Louis and Nellie Sharman. Remember those names. It's very, very important. Tell me their names and where they live."

"Louis and Nellie Sharman—but I don't want to go. No, no, I won't remember!"

"Yes, you will! I'm also going to give you the number of our Swiss bank account. There is enough money there to pay for everything you and Ellen will need." He rattled off twelve numbers. "Say them, Rena."

"I don't remember," she answered petulantly.

"Renata, listen, I'm going to get very angry. This is very important. It isn't a game we are playing!" Again, he repeated the numbers.

Renata said them correctly. She was so bright that in spite of herself, she recalled the numbers perfectly.

"Now, the names of your cousins and where they live."

"Nellie and Louis Sharman in Zurich."

All through the night, at various intervals, Gustel made

Renata repeat the information he had given her. But Renata, basking in the warmth of her mother's smile and father's laughter, hadn't given up. She nagged and pleaded to stay. Finally her Mama said, "Rena dear, listen, you know we want you with us more than anything in this world. But right now, it is impossible. Your Papa is doing things that are helping France win the war, so that someday soon, we can be together forever, so we can live in freedom and peace. If you stay, Papa would be in great danger because he would be so worried about you. We all have to do our part to win this war against Hitler. Your Papa has to do his work, and your part is to be brave, and accept the fact that you cannot be with us in France.

Renata did understand, but she definitely didn't like it. She tried to talk to her father. She had always been able to get her way with him. This was the first time she wasn't succeeding. Suddenly, an idea came to her. She was sure it would work. She looked around the room and found a pencil and paper. She thought, I am going to write a letter and make believe it came from my Oma in heaven. I know Papa loved her so much. He even named me after her. And he'll have to listen to his Mama.

She wrote:

Dear Gustel,

Even if you have to help France, you can do it if your children stay with you.

Your Mama in Heaven.

But nothing was going to change the Haberers' minds. If they could do nothing else, they were going to make sure their daughters would survive this terrible war.

All night, they stayed together, reveling in their love for each other. It was so bittersweet, because they knew they'd shortly be torn apart. The Haberers had doubts that they would survive. The work they were doing was very dangerous, and if they were captured, they would be killed. Fortunately, the girls were unaware of the true danger their parents were in. "Rena, remember what I once told you. If you are taken to church, and you probably will be, it's okay. A church is a house of God. If you ever need help, you can always ask a nun or a priest. We've heard many stories of nuns and priests helping to protect Jewish children," her mother said. It was the safest place Ruth could suggest for her girls to go if they had any problems.

"Mama, what if the girls are mean to me again? In Aspet, I was so miserable and lonely. I hated to get up everyday."

"But Rena, then you were happy in Limoges. If things are bad and you are unhappy, try to find a way to make it better. You're my brave, resourceful girl and you are able to solve your problems. I know you can."

Renata glowed under her mother's praise. Accepting now that they were not going to permit her to remain in France, she decided not to worry her parents anymore and enjoy whatever time they had left.

"Okay, I'll do my part and I'll take good care of Ellen too."

"That's my Rena. I know you will," and she held her daughter close to her.

Renata tried not to, but she simply had to tell her Mama about the chocolate. She wanted her mother to know how very much she loved her.

"Mama, I don't want to tattle, but Nicole gave Ellen and me some chocolate, and I wanted to save it for you and Papa. But Ellen ate it. I know she is little, but I did want to give it to you so much."

"My little Rena! It's enough you told me. Imagine Rena giving up sweets for us. I know, *Liebchen*, how much it meant to you, and I'll always treasure the memory. And you remember what I told you before you went to Aspet—if you're lonely, just close your eyes and Papa and I will be there with you.

The night came to an end, morning dawned. Nicole came for the children, and took them on the train to the border between France and Switzerland.

CHAPTER 14

CROSSING TO SAFETY

They reached the border in the afternoon.

"Come," said Nicole, "let us walk for a while. I have some things I need to tell you."

Ellen happily ran ahead after the long train ride. Renata started to call her back, but Nicole stopped her.

"Let her run. We can watch her and I want to tell you what will happen tonight. I don't want Ellen to know at the present time. She is too little to understand and she just might blurt it out to someone."

"Why do I have to know?"

"It's always wise to be prepared. You never know what might happen, and I promised that I would get you to Switzerland safely. We will cross the border into Switzerland once it is dark." She continued, "There are no searchlights, so we cannot easily be seen. The border guards here are Italian, and they have been bribed not to notice us. You and Ellen need to be absolutely silent the whole time. If there is any noise, they can no longer pretend that they don't see us crossing the border. I want you to keep Ellen close to you. Don't let go of her hand. Convince her that she must not utter a sound. We will run a short distance until we reach some train tracks. We must cross the tracks quickly, but carefully, because a train is expected shortly. Our escape has been planned precisely with the train's schedule. The idea is to get over the tracks before any one notices us. Then the train will block us from the guards. This is where I will leave you. You and Ellen can walk the rest of the way without worrying. There is a little path to follow on the other side of the tracks and it will take you right to the Swiss border. You will see the Swiss flag. It is a white cross on a red background. A soldier will be there, but he will be Swiss. Barbed wire is supposed to keep anyone from getting through, but you are to pick up the wire carefully so that Ellen can crawl under it. And then, you are to go through also. Is there anything you don't understand?"

"No, but—never mind." Renata had been going to protest leaving France, but she knew it would be useless to do so.

She was so unhappy. Each moment was bringing her closer and closer to leaving France. Although she hadn't been living with her parents, at least they had all been in the same country. It was a frightening thought to be in a strange county without anyone she knew. She thought, I wish I was older. Then no one could make me do things I didn't want to, she thought, forgetting how helpless the Jewish people were under Hitler's rule. She forgot how they had been torn from their homes, from their livelihoods, even from their children.

Nicole interrupted her thoughts, "We'll wander around until dinner time and I'm going to take you to a pretty little café. We won't talk about going to Switzerland anymore.

We will just pretend we are a family out for a special treat."

Dusk came and the three of them entered the café. Renata was excited. Hitler had forbidden Jews to eat in restaurants. It had been so long since she had been in one. As they were seated, she looked around. It was a charming little place, and in spite of the situation, she was pleased to be there.

"Order anything you want," Nicole said as they were handed the menus. "Not that there is much choice these days, as food is so scarce. You know, most of what we grow goes right to Germany."

They ordered what they could and in spite of the lack of selections, Renata felt quite wonderful being in a restaurant. They sat there and talked until darkness fell. Quietly, Nicole paid the bill, and taking each girl by the hand led them to where they were to cross the border. They crept through some heavy shrubbery and lay down.

"No talking," she whispered. "Be as still as mice."

It was a very black night with only a sliver of white moon to light the way. Renata could see the empty space and the silvery glitter of railway tracks ahead.

"Its almost time," Nicole whispered. Just then a **German** sentry passed! The Germans had learned that the bribed Italians were allowing people to cross to Switzerland and had replaced them with their own soldiers. Nicole, very young and terrified, gasped! She panicked! She grabbed Renata, "Run, children run! Run as fast as you can! Go to safety, but I can't go with you," and she disappeared into the night.

Renata was stunned. She didn't know what to do. She seized Ellen's hand and started to run. What am I supposed to do? Oh, yes, the train tracks—get over quickly before the train comes. She yanked Ellen's hand, but Ellen was confused and angry. She became belligerent.

"I'm not coming, I'm not! You can't make me. Don't pull me. Don't boss me," she yelled.

"Ellen, if you're not quiet the soldiers…"

"You don't know what you're talking about."

As Ellen was big for her age, and Renata small, she proved a dead weight for her sister. But Renata dragged and pulled her along. Renata was almost in tears.

What should I do? I don't want to go. I want … oh, I don't know what I want. What should I do? Just keep running, she told herself. Don't think … just run! As Ellen kept pulling her back, and continued her loud grumbling, Renata thought, she'll get us both killed! I hate her! I hate her! I wish I could just leave her. But no, Mama and Papa would never forgive me if I left her. And I probably would never forgive myself.

In a soft voice, she coaxed "Come on, come on Ellen. Be good."

All at once, they heard a voice. A soldier speaking German shouted, "Halt or I'll shoot!"

Renata's heart stopped beating. What should I do now? Keep running, keep running! But Ellen, who had been in France since she was two, couldn't understand German. She had completely forgotten the language. All she knew was that it sounded like her Papa. She said, "It's Papa. It is Papa. I'm going to him."

"It's not Papa. That man is going to kill you!"

"No…"

Renata pulled harder. She was almost at the train tracks, only a little further to go, but the weight of her sister caused her to fall on the tracks, and she split her knee wide open. Stones from the tracks became embedded in the open wound. Blood gushed forth. The pain was agonizing and she started to cry. How could she go on? Part of her wanted to lie there and give up. But the train was coming.

If she didn't get up instantly, the train would kill her. Knowing what she had to do, she got to her feet. Though still grumbling, seeing her sister cry, Ellen relented and allowed Renata to pull her across the tracks. The German was able to cross the tracks as well.

The soldier followed the girls all the way to the Swiss border. Every few minutes, he called, "Halt or I will shoot!" But he never raised his gun. He was so close, Renata could feel his breath on her back, but he never touched them.

Maybe he had children of his own. Maybe, he simply had a kind heart and wasn't up to waging war on children. But, if they had stopped, he would have had no choice but to take them back to German-occupied France.

Renata and Ellen reached the Swiss border. Renata saw the barbed wire, saw the red flag with the white cross in the center. She saw a sign that said Suisse. She relaxed, but suddenly she saw the soldier standing there on the Swiss border. He was wearing a German uniform! Nicole had not thought to mention that the Swiss and Germans wore very similar uniforms.

What should I do now? I don't know what to do. I can't go back. I'll just have to go on. She took Ellen, whom she hated passionately at the moment, knocked her down as hard as she could and pushed her under the barbed wire. "Now just go!" For once, Ellen didn't say anything. She swiftly crawled through. Ellen was safe in Switzerland. Now it was Renata's turn She tried to follow Ellen, but she was exhausted. Her knee was throbbing achingly, and because of her knee she couldn't bend low enough to creep under the wire. She was caught…caught on the sharp points of the wire! The more she struggled to free herself, the more entangled she got. The pain in her knee was now excruciating. Blood was gushing out; she was helpless. It was all over. She simply gave up. She lay there like a little animal caught in a trap.

Ellen looked at her sister. She began to weep. "Rena, Rena, I'm sorry, please, Rena don't get killed. Crawl, crawl like I did. Don't leave me, don't...please Rena, please, Rena."

The Swiss soldier saw what was happening. He looked at the German standing there. The German looked at him. The Swiss sentry knew that if he stepped on French soil, he could be shot. But he couldn't stand there and watch a child be captured. There must be an excellent reason why two little girls would be crossing the border alone. He opened the gate, stared at the German, and calmly untangled Renata, lifted her in his arms and carried her to safety.

The German soldier turned and walked back to his post.

CHAPTER 15

SWITZERLAND

Renata thought about her life since she arrived in Switzerland.

The two girls were taken to Camp de Camilles in Geneva. Anyone who crossed the border illegally was brought to this detention camp to be debriefed. When they were brought there and questioned, Renata told the authorities she had cousins in Zurich and also that she had the number of her father's Swiss bank account. Pleased that the two girls would not be a burden to the Swiss government, the authorities informed Renata that they would try to locate her relatives. Ellen was taken to the children's section of the camp, but Renata was put in the hospital. The torn knee, embedded with stones, had rapidly become badly infected. She would have this large scar for the rest of her life.

Renata loved being in the hospital. She lay in a clean, white bed in a sun filled room. The nurses were extremely kind to the brave young girl who had crossed the border, while bringing her little sister with her. They brought her wonderful Swiss chocolates to eat and books to read. For the first time in years, she was not only being taken care of, but was being catered to. She didn't have to think, to plan, to act. She wished she could stay there forever, or at least until the war was over and she could again be with her parents.

Ellen felt differently. She wanted her big sister with her. Everyday, she would be brought to the hospital to visit Renata and she would demand, "When are you going to be better?" But Renata only smiled, and when Ellen would leave, she would continue her reading. The nurses had introduced her to the books of Johanna Spyri, the Swiss author. She especially loved the book Heidi. When she had read all of the children's books the hospital owned, they brought her adult books. She was perfectly content to lie there and read. It didn't matter what she was reading; she was living in a warm, safe cocoon.

However, nothing lasts forever. Her knee did heal, and in December, 1942, just before her tenth birthday, Renata and Ellen were sent to a children's home in Ascona. They were to remain there until the authorities managed to locate their relatives. A wonderful woman, Lilly Volkhart, ran the home in Ascona. This children's home had originally been a profitable private boarding school, but when Jewish refugee children started to enter Switzerland alone, this warm-hearted and generous woman had opened her door to them. It was a lovely place. Renata found that Eva and Miriam Cohen, her friends from Offenburg, were among the children who had found their way there. Renata would have been content to stay there, but her cousins were eventually located.

Another move! In April, Renata and Ellen were sent to

Zurich. The Sharmans felt that it would be too difficult to take on the care of two extra children, so the sisters were separated. Renata remained with the Sharmans, while Ellen was sent to another cousin. A few months later, Frau Sharman became ill, and in addition, the other cousin became pregnant. These cousins were no longer willing to take on the responsibility for these small victims of Hitler's Germany.

In addition, news had begun filtering in that the Jews, in the occupied countries, were being sent to killing centers. The Sharmans were afraid that Ruth and Gustel Haberer would be killed, leaving them to care for Renata and Ellen until they were adults. There was little sympathy for the two lonely children. It was decided to send them to boarding schools. The money Herr Haberer had in his bank account was sufficient to pay for their school fees. Due to the girls' age difference, sadly, they were sent to separate schools. If Ruth and Gustel didn't survive the war, the girls were to remain at the boarding schools until they reached the age of eighteen. At the time, it seemed highly unlikely that their parents would survive.

So, thought Renata, here I am in the town of Arth-Goldau, with Fraulein Eichorn and her terrible temper. I can't stand it, and this could go on forever. What can I do? Think, she told herself. Mama told me I could always find a solution if I tried. The problem remained with her until the morning Fraulein Eichorn sent her on an errand to the town of Arth-Goldau. Whenever an errand had to be done, the Fraulein would send Renata. Renata was one of the few children in the school who had been born in Germany, and thus was able to speak German fluently. Not only could she speak German, but due to the fact that she picked up languages so easily, she now could also speak *Schweizerdeutsch.* This was a difficult dialect, spoken by the

Swiss.

The Fraulein also knew, and Renata knew as well, that she wouldn't be missing much in the Fraulein's classroom. All she was teaching was *Schweizerdeutsch*. School had become really boring for Renata. Whereas in Aspet and Limoges, school had provided an interest for her, here she was learning nothing at all. She usually had a book hidden under her desk, which she would surreptitiously read. Renata knew this wasn't right. She knew that she had to be educated. She remembered how her mother had sent her to Freiburg, because that was the closest Jewish school available. Mama had insisted that she attend the school set up in Gurs. Her mother had told her that getting educated was a child's job.

Still pondering her problem of living at the boarding school, she reached the town. Her eyes took in the beautiful little village. It was surrounded by the mountain Rigi. There were small, red-roof houses that looked like the places in Johanna Spyri books. And there stood a beautiful Catholic church. Renata had an idea!

Recalling that her Mama had told her that nuns were good people, she sat down on the church steps and waited for someone to come along. In the interim, she reflected on her life—how alone she was, how far she was from her Mama and Papa—and she started to cry. For a little girl who had rarely cried, now the tears always seemed ready to flow.

Deep in her despair, she never saw the nun approach. "Are you waiting for someone?" the nun kindly asked.

"For you," Renata answered.

"Do you know me?" The nun was surprised.

"No, I don't know your name, but I do know that nuns are good people."

Gazing at the tear stained face, Sister Berta said, "What

is it, child?"

"I have no mother and I have no father. I'm Jewish and I'm so very unhappy. But I know, because my Mama told me, that nuns are good and I want to come and stay with you because you won't be mean like Fraulein Eichorn."

"Tell me about it. Are you living at the school with Fraulein Eichorn?"

"Yes, and she is so mean sometimes. She hits ..."

"Has she hit you?"

"No, not me, but she does hit my friends and she yells all the time."

"Do you children deserve it?"

"I don't know," said Renata honestly. "Sometimes we probably do. I guess the Fraulein isn't really mean; she did make arrangements for me to climb Mt. Rigi, and she does give me books from her own library to read. Maybe she just doesn't have patience for children, especially if they don't speak good Swiss German."

"I see you speak good Swiss German," the nun smiled.

"Yes, you see, I was born in Germany, so I had no trouble learning Swiss German. The others come from Poland and Italy, so it is much harder for them. I guess that's why the Fraulein is nicer to me. I'm not getting a good education. And my Mama always told me education was very important."

"Doesn't Fraulein Eichorn have classes?"

"Well, she usually just teaches German and since I know it, I get bored."

"What do you do then?"

Renata felt embarrassed, but felt obliged to tell the truth.

She sighed, and said, "I take a book and keep it on my lap and read while she teaches. She does have a lot of good books to read."

"Now that doesn't sound like a good idea to me," said

Sister Berta. "You stay here while I talk to the Reverend Mother."

Renata sat quietly until the nun returned.

"The Reverend Mother will see you now."

Renata went with Sister Berta to the office. She curtsied and when the head of the convent said, "Tell me, child, what troubles you?" Renata's eyes filled with tears again and she started to retell her story.

"I have no Mama and I have no Papa. I'm all alone and I'm very unhappy."

"What would make you happy?"

"I'd like to come and live with you and go to your school."

"That is impossible. We don't have children living here. This is a day school."

"Could I at least go to your school then?"

"I don't know. We would have to speak to Fraulein Eichorn. The other children's parents pay for them and I don't know if Fraulein Eichorn will pay for you."

Renata wasn't too worried. She was sure something could be worked out.

"Would you mind if I told the Fraulein what you told sister Berta and me?" the Reverend Mother asked Renata.

"I'd rather not get in trouble, but if that's the only way that I can go to school here, then tell her."

The Reverend Mother thought, if the child is willing for me to speak to Fraulein Eichorn, she must be very unhappy—unhappy enough to take a chance of being punished. Aloud, she said, "You go home now, and I'll see what I can do."

That evening, the Fraulein called Renata to her office. "The Reverend Mother called me and I hear you want to go to the Catholic school. Why do you want to do that? You know, you'll have a long walk everyday and it's terribly cold and snowy in the winter. Here you just have to go to another room for your classes."

"Remember Fraulein when you took me to church one Sunday and I liked it so much. It made me feel so good, so I'd really like to go to Catholic school."

The Fraulein smiled, "I guess it can be arranged. The Reverend Mother said that she will accept you as a scholarship student. I know you will get a good education because I went there myself."

Renata was thrilled. Things became even better than she expected. Because Renata loved to sing, she usually sang on her way to school. One day, the priest who also loved to sing, overheard her.

"Would you like to come to early mass?" he asked her.

"Oh yes, I love the singing in Church," she replied.

The priest, knowing Renata had such a long walk to school each morning, asked if she would like to have breakfast after Mass with him. What a joy! The priest's housekeeper was a great cook and prepared wonderful breakfasts. So everyday Renata attended early Mass and ate breakfast with the Priest. In addition, each time she attended early Mass, she would receive a holy card (small devotional pictures depicting religious scenes or saints). After a child accumulated ten holy cards, they would get a special treat. Renata felt as if she were in heaven.

Renata was now eleven and a half. For the first time in three years, she felt as if she had a place where she belonged. She enjoyed her studies, and best of all, she had made very good friends. The one she liked most was Clara. Renata was very taken with her. She thought this girl was wonderful. She was full of mischievous ideas and always getting into trouble. She never ever worried about the consequences of her actions. Renata was envious of her freedom to just be herself. Clara dawdled on her way to school and arrived late. At recess, she stayed outside too long. Once, she brought her brother's pet mouse to school and released it under the teacher's desk. What a riot that had caused! The nuns were exasperated and were always informing her that she would not go to heaven. This troubled Clara, but not enough to stop her behavior. One day, however, she went too far.

The Monsignor was visiting the school and all the children lined up to greet him. He took each child's hand and blessed them. When Clara's turn came, she gave him her hand which she had blackened with charcoal. He then put his hand on his face and left a long black smudge on his cheek. The children couldn't contain their giggles. The nuns were furious.

Back in the classroom, Sister Maria called Clara to the front of the room. "Now you have done it. You are a disgrace to your parents and to the school. You are definitely not going to heaven."

Clara was really worried this time. She wasn't a bad child, just an extremely mischievous one. She began to sob. But, Sister Maria was not moved. Renata felt sorry for her and when Clara passed her desk, she whispered to her, "Don't worry, I will save you a place in Jewish heaven."

Sister Maria heard. "Renata, first of all, no one saves places in heaven. Also, what makes you so sure you're going to heaven?"

"Oh, I'm going," she answered firmly. Renata was not concerned. She knew she always tried to be good. Besides, she felt the good Lord was not too good to her for most of her life. He owed her.

That day, Clara went home and told her mother how nice Renata was to her. Of course, she didn't tell what she had done, but her parents were happy that Clara had made a good friend. Clara and her family were Lutheran, not

Catholic. Her parents were sending her to the Catholic school because it was the best school in the area. The children had not been too friendly to her because she was not Catholic. Her parents were so pleased that their daughter finally had a friend that they started to invite Renata to their house. Sometimes she went on trips with Clara's family. Renata was fairly content with her life. Life was pleasant, or as pleasant as it could be without her family.

Before falling asleep every night, she would bring forth the warm memory of her family sitting around the table, drinking hot chocolate and eating crusty white rolls. She was sure that one day they would be together again.

CHAPTER 16

1945

Time marches on. The days turned into weeks, the weeks into months, the months into years. Renata had been in Switzerland for two and a half years. She wasn't unhappy, but she wasn't quite happy either. She felt as if she was marking time until she could be back with her parents. She enjoyed her friends, her school, and the magnificence of the Swiss countryside. She never heard from her parents, but then again, she didn't expect to. She had gotten used to that emptiness when she was in Aspet. She kept her belief that they were alive and well.

One day in April, however, her awareness changed. Fraulein Eichorn called her to the office. A telegram had come for her. Anxiously, she tore it open, wondering who had sent it. Quickly, she scanned to the bottom. It was from her beloved Aunt Martha and Uncle Ludwig who had emigrated to South Africa long ago.

Dear Renata,

Your Uncle and I have been trying to locate you for the past three years. The Red Cross finally found you in Arth-Goldau. We want you to know how much we love you. Renata, no matter what happens, you and Ellen will never be alone. You will always have a home with us. As soon as the war is over, we will be able to bring you to South Africa.

Love from your Aunt Martha and Uncle Ludwig

Renata threw the telegram to the floor in absolute fury. "What do they mean? How dare they? They think Mama and Papa are dead. I know they are alive. I'll be with them. I will! I will!"

She broke into shuddering sobs. She didn't want to face the fact that her parents may have been captured and killed. "No, no," she wept. Fraulein Eichorn put her arms around Renata for the first time in all the years she had been in the school. But, Renata pushed her away. She ran to her room, flung herself on her bed and cried and cried. She wept until there were no tears left. Still trembling, she thought of her sweet aunt and uncle. She recalled how much she had loved them and had even tried to prevent them from leaving Germany. In spite of herself, she realized how good they were to think of her. Renata finally did take comfort that there was someone in the world who really did love and want her.

The war in Europe was coming to an end. The Allies had invaded France June 6, 1944, and on May 8, 1945, the German Army surrendered.

Gustel and Ruth Haberer had survived and had done

their part in the defeat of Hitler's Germany. The Underground acknowledged their brave deeds and asked them where they would like to live. They had no wish to return to Germany. Their memories of that land were too bitter. They didn't want to remain in Brives. Some of the French people had collaborated with the Germans, and Gustel felt it would not be a safe haven for his children. Besides, the Haberers wanted their own name and identity back. Herr Haberer contacted the OSE and asked if they had a job for him. A Children's Home in St. Etienne, France, needed someone to be in charge of their purchasing. In addition, they could use his wife to do the sewing and even had a job for Oma. She could help in the kitchen. The Haberers decided it was the best place at this time until a permanent decision for their future could be made.

Tracing where their daughters were now, they made plans for their return to France. In June, Renata received another telegram, but this time, she let out a shriek of joy when she saw the bottom. The wondrous words were Mama and Papa and Oma.

Dearest Renata,

Our greatest prayers have been answered. Just as we promised you, at last we are going to be together. We can't wait to hold you in our arms. It has been so very long since we've seen you. Arrangements have been made with Fraulein Eichorn and our cousins to get you and Ellen to St. Etienne. We will be at the station waiting for you. Rena, it will be just a few more days until we are together.

All our love, Mama, Papa and Oma

Joy radiated throughout Renata's body. Her Mama, her Papa, her Oma—she was going home! She was going home! In just two days, she would be leaving Arthe-

Goldau, barely enough time for her farewells. The next morning, she could hardly contain her happiness as she made her morning's journey to school. The sky was so blue, the sun so bright, the morning filled with joy, but none of it could even approach the lightheartedness that filled every pore of her body.

"Father," she said, a smile lighting her face when she arrived at the church, "I'm going home."

"Home, and where is that?"

"Home, home is where my Mama and Papa and Oma are."

"You're right, Renata. I will miss our mornings, but I am very happy for you. God bless you and keep you."

When she told the news to her friends, Clara said, "What will I do without you? I'll miss you so much."

But Renata couldn't be sad. Her whole body kept singing, I'm going home, I'm going home. I'm going to see my Mama and Papa and Oma too, she kept repeating to herself.

It was almost three years since the children had last seen their parents. Renata was almost thirteen and Ellen was nearly nine. Ellen was brought to Arth-Goldau and then, Fraulein Eichorn put them both on a train to Zurich. The Sharmans would take charge of the rest of their journey. The Sharmans bought a new wardrobe for each of the girls, realizing that clothes would be hard to find in newly liberated France. Then they crossed the border, not secretly and not dangerously, but openly and safely, and the two girls boarded a train bound for France. Renata could scarcely keep her happiness in check. Mama, Papa, and Oma too, Mama, Papa and Oma too, the train wheels seemed to be saying. She suddenly noticed Ellen's face. She looked so unhappy. Her eyes were scared.

"Ellen, what is the matter?"

"I don't remember Mama and Papa. I don't know what they look like! What if I don't know them?" and she started to cry. "I don't know my own Mama and Papa,"

"You will, Ellen. Don't worry. I know you will."

"But I won't! I can't remember them, I can't," she sobbed.

"I'll point them out to you. I promise, Ellen. Please don't cry." And all through the trip, Renata kept comforting her sister.

The conductor called, "St. Etienne next." Ellen and Renata stood up to walk to the door of the train. It was a beautiful, warm June day. The windows of the train were open, and a soft breeze of summer air wafted in. The train screeched its whistle as it entered the station. Renata anxiously scanned the platform. Her eyes found three people standing together. There was a lovely, dark haired woman poised in front of a tall man. Holding on to his arm, was a small older woman. Tears started down Renata's cheeks as a smile lit up her face. As she turned to tell Ellen, there was a shout—a shout of dreams fulfilled, a shout that made every person recall the happiest moment of their lives. A shout from Ellen, "Mama."

But Renata just stood there, happiness enveloping her, as she whispered, "Mama, Papa and Oma too."

POSTSCRIPT

After the war ended, the Haberers remained in France for two years. The OSE gave Ruth and Gustel jobs at L'Allouette Children's Home, doing work similar to what they had done at the Munich Jewish Children's Home.

Their happiness was checked by the news they received, that Opa had been murdered in Maidanek. Also, a great many of their relatives and friends were murdered in various camps in Poland.

However, their cousin Robert Weil and his family had found refuge in the United States.

In March of 1947, Oma left for South Africa to join

her other daughter Martha and son-in-law Ludwig. She had not seen them since 1935, when they had left for South Africa.

Four months later, the Haberers left for the United States. Before leaving, Gustel went to visit Germany one last time. Ruth refused to go—she had vowed never again to set foot on German soil. While there, Gustel met with one of his oldest and dearest friends, Willie Wussler. Herr Wussler was a contractor and owned a warehouse. After their happy reunion, Herr Wussler took Gustel to the back of his warehouse. Willie removed some heavy blankets that were covering twelve crates that he had hidden for Gustel for the past ten years. He explained to Gustel that he knew that if one man were to return from the war it would be him. Herr Wussler shipped the crates to Chicago free of charge. He said this was part of a debt no one could ever repay. These crates contained family treasures as well as photos of the family.

In June of 1947, the Haberers left for the United States. They were immediately embraced by the extended family of Robert and Herta Weil.

By 1950, the Haberers were content and comfortable in their new country. Ruth and Gustel both had jobs, Ruth as a designer at a dress company, and Gustel as a maintenance engineer. Ellen was happy and doing well in school. Renata (now known as Renee) was granted a scholarship at Katherine Gibbs School of Business.

In 1951, tragedy struck again, when Ruth was diagnosed with cancer. She passed away in 1952 at the age of 42.

Gustel died in 1961 at the age of 64.

Ellen moved to South Africa in 1960 at the age of 23, to be with the other side of her family. She married and had a son, Jean Marc. Sadly, she also died of cancer at the young age of 40 in 1977.

Oma died in her sleep in November 1964.

Renee married Dr. Thomas Krauss in December 1964. Cousin Robert walked her down the aisle. While the Krausses never had children, the children and grandchildren of their extended family filled their hearts.

Renee had a very successful thirty-year career at Budget Rent a Car as Director of Global Sales Analysis.

Renee died in January 2014, at 81 years of age.

Renata

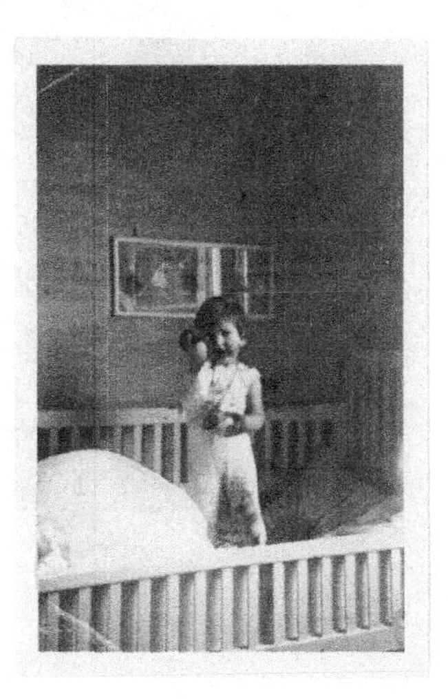

Ellen

Gustel and Ellen

Renata and Ellen

Ellen and Renata
circa 1945

Ellen and Renata
circa 1945

Renata, Ruth, Ellen and Gustel
circa 1945

Ruth Haberer

Gustel Haberer

Uncle Ludwig and
Aunt Martha
South Africa 1955

Renata and Ellen
circa 1950

Ellen and Renata

Ellen, Oma, Aunt Martha and Uncle Ludwig in South Africa

Ellen and Gerard

Renata (Renee) and
Thomas Krauss

ABOUT THE BOOK
BY HELEN STEIN BEHR

I met Renee at one of the Weils' extended family Seders. When the Haggadah (the recited text for the Seder) came to the part when the Jewish slaves escaped across the Red Sea, Renee began relating to me her odyssey crossing the border to Switzerland. When she mentioned her age of nine and that she'd also been responsible for her five-year-old sister, I felt that this story should be told.

After I got to know Renee better, I asked if she would be interested in my writing a novel about her experiences growing up during the Holocaust. She was enthusiastic about the idea, and I suggested that I tape her memories.

In addition, I researched the years of 1930 to 1945 at several Holocaust libraries, as well as the history of German life before that time. I fell in love with Ruth and Gustel Haberer as well as with the brave Renata. I hope you fell in love with them as well.

Made in the USA
Monee, IL
23 March 2020